WHAT THEY DON'T KNOW

ANITA HORROCKS

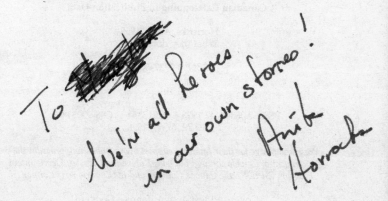

To ~~[scribbled out]~~

We're all Heroes
in our own stories!

Anita
Horrocks

Stoddart Kids

TORONTO • NEW YORK

Published in Canada in 1998 by
Stoddart Kids,
a division of Stoddart Publishing Co. Ltd.
34 Lesmill Road
Toronto, Canada M3B 2T6
Tel (416) 445-3333 Fax (416) 445-5967
E-mail cservice@genpub.com

Published in the United States in 1999 by
Stoddart Kids,
a division of Stoddart Publishing Co. Ltd.
180 Varick Street, 9th Floor
New York, New York 10014
Toll free 1-800-805-1083
E-mail gdsinc@genpub.com

Distributed in Canada by
General Distribution Services
325 Humber College Blvd.
Toronto, Canada M9W 7C3
Tel (416) 213-1919 Fax (416) 213-1917
E-mail cservice@genpub.com

Distributed in the United States by
General Distribution Services, PMB 128
4500 Witmer Industrial Estates
Niagara Falls, New York 14305-1386
Toll free 1-800-805-1083
E-mail gdsinc@genpub.com

04 03 02 01 00   2 3 4 5

Canadian Cataloguing in Publication Data

Horrocks, Anita, 1958–
What they don't know

ISBN: 0-7737-6001-6

I. Title.

PS8565.0686W42 1998   jC813'.54   C98-930514-7
PZ7.H67Wh 1998

*We acknowledge for their financial support of our publishing program the
Government of Canada through the Book Publishing Industry Development
Program (BPIDP), the Canada Council, and the Ontario Arts Council.*

Cover and text design: Tannice Goddard
Cover Illustration: Janet Wilson

Printed and bound in Canada

Acknowledgments

I would like to thank the professionals who so helpfully provided medical and legal information, including Dr. Vincent Hanlon, Mr. Kieran Biggins and Ms. Diane Shanks of the Lethbridge Regional Hospital, Dr. Garnette R. Sutherland of Calgary's Foothills Hospital, Chief John LaFlamme of the City of Lethbridge Police Service, Mr. Barry Horner, Chief Probation Officer with the Community Corrections Branch of Alberta Justice, and Ms. Rhonda Ruston, Solicitor. Any technical errors or inconsistencies are mine alone. Thanks also to the many individuals who helped produce the various drafts of letters, handwritten notes and other document facsimiles contained in this novel, including Amy, Erin, Kathy and Garth Sherwin, Ali, Robin, Kathy and Doug Hopkins, Bryan Horrocks, Lindsay Horrocks, Brian and Betty Bourassa, Sandra and Gil Tourigny, Diane Lievers, Jeff Warren, Fiona Randle, Kim King, Tess McCallum and Phil Conroy, along with members of the Lethbridge Senior Citizen's Organization — Executive Director Dennis Dray, Jean Matthews, Albert Cheesman, Helen Balaz, Joan McDonald, Ann Cameron, Mildred Byrne, Anne Hryvnak and Norma Langford.

The documents, events and characters in this novel are fictional. The city of Black Diamond bears no resemblance to the actual town of Black Diamond.

I would like to acknowledge the keen and patient editing of Sheila Dalton, along with the input and suggestions of many friends and colleagues: Marty Oordt, Blair McMurren,

Ali and Robin Hopkins, Erin Sherwin, Iris Loewen, Michael Pollard, Ian McAdam, Julie Diemert, Donovan Conley, Leona King and Ruth Klinkhammer.

I benefited tremendously from the perspective each of you brought to the original manuscript. And I will always be thankful for a most gracious publisher, Kathryn Cole, whose warmth and encouragement have given my writing career the best start I could have hoped for.

So many fine books and authors have influenced my life and my writing; I am especially indebted in this novel to those whose own opening phrases inspired and are quoted in the first chapter. They include *Autumn Street* by Lois Lowry, *Peter Pan* by James Barrie, *Who is Francis Rain?* by Margaret Buffie, *Hero of Lesser Causes* by Julie Johnston, *Catcher in the Rye* by J. D. Salinger, *Hard Times* by Charles Dickens, and *Billy Boy* by Monica Hughes.

Financial support for the writing of this novel was provided by the Alberta Foundation for the Arts, a beneficiary of Alberta Lotteries.

To Becky and Lindsay
Two heroes

"The connotation of courage,
which we now feel to be an indispensable
quality of the hero, is in fact already present in a willingness
to act and speak at all, to insert one's self into the world
and begin a story of one's own."

— H. Arendt, THE HUMAN CONDITION

Caryn & Kelly

   Sorry I ditched you
at the hospital. I
couldn't take it, waiting
like that. I can't go back
there to just sit & wait.
I have to DO something.
I have some stuff to
take care of anyway
I can't explain now. It's
a long story.
   Dad will be okay, he has
to be. If he wakes up before
I get back, tell him - Just tell
him I'll be back
         Gotta Go Hannah

1

I pull Hannah's crumpled note out of my pocket and look at it and remember that night and I think, this is one more piece to add to the others I found in Hannah's box. The pieces tell a story and a story might hold everything together.

Stories can do that, can't they? Give life a shape you can at least partly see, when what it wants to do is fly off in bits anywhere and everywhere until nothing is left at the center.

Oh, *that's* what I feel, *that's* what I need to do, *that's* who I am.

I'm sitting on the roof outside my window, sleepy sunshine licking at the light film of frost that touched down in the night, soaking the cedar shakes and me in warmth. The farmer's field behind our house deserted, stubbled with bristly shorn stalks. All that's left after the harvest. Stubbled like my father's head that they shaved so they could drill a hole in his skull.

The nighthawks are gone. Now what? Stories, after all, can begin at the end, which is maybe not the end you thought it was when you get back to the end again. Or it is.

There are so many different beginnings.

"It was a long time ago . . ."

It *feels* like a long time ago. The last week alone belongs in a whole other world, as if ordinary, every-day life can be put on hold while people get sucked into some kind of surreal commercial break. Time collapses into seconds, each one focused and distinct, sharp enough to slice you open if you make the smallest slip. Everything happens in a space framed by the beat of a father's pulse as he lies unconscious in a hospital room. And by the bigger frame of what goes before and what comes after.

"Once upon a time . . ."

Once upon a time there was a girl named Hannah who kept her secrets in a box. One day her sister, Kelly, opened the box and let all the secrets out.

Most of the story is about Hannah, after all, not me. She's the one solidly at the center of things while I watch from around the edges.

At least that's the way it was. Until what happened to Dad. Until Hannah ran, and all she left was a note. I confess to snooping, to reading Hannah's secrets, which brought me in far enough that I can't go back anymore. Not that I'm sorry exactly. But I've lost where I am and have to find my place all over again because the story changes when you move.

Hannah would do a better job of telling it. She has a flair for the dramatic, and even if her version might not resemble anyone else's, it would be a good story. But even I know that a beginning like "Once upon a time" begs to end with "and they lived happily ever after."

One day I will feel happy again. I know in my head this is true. My heart answers . . . *no guarantees, offer expires after thirty days, void where you lose who you are*.

There are other ways to begin. One of my favorites — "All children, except one, grow up . . ."

I was Peter Pan, the one child who never had to grow up. Was Hannah? Was everyone? But then I did, because all people have to, sooner or later. Sometimes it happens so quickly we don't even realize we've done it.

There are plenty of different beginnings in the stories lining the bookcase in my room upstairs in our house, the house that is Hannah's and Dad's and mine and now Caryn's, too. That much I know.

"Every first of July since I can remember . . ."

"It started off as a peaceful, plodding kind of summer . . ."

"If you really want to hear about it . . ."

"Now, what I want is, Facts . . ."

Some stories plunge you into the middle of things. "The boy ran along the street" could just as well be *Hannah ran out the door and disappeared into the night*. My sister, the prodigal daughter. I've looked up how that story starts in Luke. "A certain man had two sons . . ."

I like that. *A certain man had two daughters*. Not just any man, a certain man. Dad was — is — as certain as they come. Hannah would like it, too. Doesn't the prodigal son get to live it up until he's wasted and has stomped all over everyone, and then his father is so happy to see him he throws a party when he comes home? I know why the other son was angry.

Question: When is a father no longer a father? When he is dead? Wrong. When he's not yours? Wrong again.

At school kids tell stories that start, *"Did you hear what happened to . . .?"* or *"You should have been in third period today. It was a riot."*

Did you hear what happened to my sister, Hannah? She was arrested.

Go to jail. Go directly to jail. Do not pass go. Do not collect two hundred dollars.

You should have been at our house this Thanksgiving weekend. My little sister took off and my dad nearly died. Really.

But except for Dad's accident, what happened that weekend started long before Thanksgiving. When I think about it, the accident wouldn't have happened at all if other stuff hadn't happened first. I mean, Dad wouldn't have been on that road if Hannah hadn't told him to go, and he wouldn't even have been able to take that job in British Columbia if he hadn't married Caryn, and he couldn't have married Caryn if he and Mom weren't divorced, and — how far back is the beginning of things?

These are the fireworks that explode and sizzle through your head when a piece of your father's brain has been cut out and thrown out and your sister runs away with his heart. Hey diddle, diddle.

"In the beginning . . ."

Now that's way back, but if God created heaven and earth, didn't He have to be around already? Maybe there is no such thing as the one and only beginning. Maybe it's all just one huge long story, one long chain reaction going on forever — a sort of infinite game of dominoes.

I suppose if you never really know where something begins, let alone where it ends, just about any beginning will do. So.

In Hannah's box of secrets I found a battered and torn poster from her science fair project last February. I found a lot of things, but the poster reminds me it was at the science fair that Hannah's story, which began who knows when, first screamed to be heard.

BLOODY FACTS!

(Or everything you wanted to know about blood but were too pale to ask)

♡ Blood is multi-talented ~ it carries O_2 and CO_2, it collects garbage, it's the body's central heating and cooling system, it fights disease, makes repairs and more.

♡ Blood has all kinds of parts. Liquid plasma, red blood cells, white blood cells and platelets.

♡ White blood cells play defense. They devour old cells and bacteria, sometimes it kills them and that's what makes pus!

♡ Red blood cells carry oxygen. The book says they look like tiny donuts but we think they look more like rolled up condoms. See?

♡ Platelets help blood clot. Without platelets you could get a tiny cut and just bleed and bleed and bleed . . .

♡ You inherit blood type from your parents. You can have type A, B, AB or O. (See chart.) If you got a transfusion of the wrong type your blood could go all clumpy. It could kill you.

♡ Your body holds about six litres of blood and your heart pumps between 5 000 and 6 000 litres of blood every day. That's like a hundred tanks of gas!

2

The school gymnasium was swarming with kids and parents when Mom and I arrived. A steady drone of conversation hovered about the crowd, interrupted by the occasional buzz, bang or whistle.

While we were getting our bearings, there was a loud poof and a gasp from a small group of people gathered around one display. Smoke began to billow above their heads, a boy came running down the aisle. "Gangway!" he yelled, grabbing a fire extinguisher from the wall near the door, pivoting smoothly and running back. He pointed and squeezed the trigger, smothering a small fire in a chemical cloud. The crowd applauded.

Mom raised her eyebrows. "Is this sort of thing common?"

I shrugged. "It's a science fair. There's always at least one explosion."

Mom shook her head and scanned the room. "It's a zoo in here. How do we find Hannah's display?"

"Follow me. Maybe we can spot her if we walk down that middle aisle." I had no desire to spend any time looking at erupting volcanoes, Styrofoam models of the solar system, or the sexual organs of flowers. I'd done the junior high science fair thing. Besides, I didn't often get Mom to myself. I just wanted to find Hannah's display, give her a pat on the back and get out of there.

Mom was the one who insisted on dropping by for a few minutes before we went out to dinner and a movie. "I don't get a chance to go to many of these things, Kelly," she said. "But that doesn't mean I'm not interested. Hannah went to the trouble of sending me an invitation. It must be important to her."

She'd even brought her camera. But then, Mom rarely went anywhere without her camera. It's just that not many of her photos were of her kids. Mom was right about one thing — she didn't have much of a presence at our activities. Hannah spent two years in Girl Guides and Mom never made an outing. She'd missed my photo club's exhibit the month before; it was the first time I'd shown my photos in public. Hannah was just lucky that Mom happened to be in town this week.

I was being unfair, I knew. It was frustrating for Mom, too. She couldn't help it if famous photojournalists were away a lot. Well, maybe Mom wasn't exactly famous, but Maddie Farrell's photos had won awards and appeared in *National Geographic* and *Life*. Which is why we lived with Dad. With Dad and Caryn now.

The crowd was thick in the main aisle and I jostled against someone's shoulder. "Sorry," I muttered. The someone turned and I recognized Sean Erais from school. Sean was in most of my honors classes, and was on the track and cross-country teams.

He grinned at me and moved aside to let us pass. "My humblest apologies, Kelly. I would never want to be the one to get in your way. I've seen you run."

I blushed and hurried past him, wondering how Sean knew that I ran. Mom raised her eyebrows at me.

"Just a guy from school," I said. Then I spotted Hannah and Kyle. The two of them were hard to miss. Their backdrop was blood red, and they were made up like vampires. They looked like they belonged at a Halloween party, not a science fair.

"Over there," I nodded, pulling Mom along.

Hannah wore a long, straight black wig over her shoulder-length dark brown hair. Kyle's black hair was slicked back. He looked passable, but Hannah made a great vampire with her high cheekbones, arched eyebrows and full lips painted blood red. Her skin held its tan all year, and her cheeks were a little too plump maybe — a bit healthy-looking for one of the undead. But the overall effect was sort of exotic, especially when her green, almost–emerald eyes flashed. Like they were flashing now at the group of little kids gathered around their display.

"Ugh!" One of the kids grimaced. "No way I'm gonna let you stab me."

"Do it yourself then," Hannah said. "It's just a little poke. Do you want to know your blood type or not?" She handed him a small metal instrument with a sharp point on the end, the same kind they use in clinics to prick your finger.

The kid barely stuck himself with the metal point. Hannah rolled her eyes. "Are you sure you broke the skin?" she asked. She squeezed his finger hard to get a couple of drops of blood onto two slides.

"Ow!" the kid protested.

Hannah ignored him, handing the slides to Kyle. Both of them were wearing plastic gloves. Kyle used eye droppers to put a few drops of blue liquid on one slide and drops of yellow liquid on the other. He tilted the slides back and forth to mix the liquids and then set them on the table.

"Now watch," he told the kids.

"How does it work?" one of them asked.

"Read the chart," Hannah said. She sighed and pointed at the display behind her. "See, it says right there. Blood has these things called antigens. If you have A antigens, you have type A blood. If you have B antigens, you have type B blood. If you have both, you have type AB. And if you have neither, you have type O. Simple."

Kyle jumped in. "See the blood on this slide, the one with the blue stuff? See how it's starting to get little speckles in it, like dust?"

The kid shook his head. "I don't see it."

"Here. Look under the microscope." Kyle put the slide under the microscope for him. "Now can you see it?"

"Oh, yeah. My blood's got little clumps in it. They're growing!"

"That means you have the A antigen in your blood. But the slide with the yellow stuff isn't doing that. It just looks normal because you don't have any B antigen. So your blood type is probably type A."

"Probably?"

"Well," Kyle explained. "This is just a kind of shortcut test. It's pretty good and it's probably right, but to be a hundred percent certain you'd have to have a real lab do the test."

The kid looked confused. "Why would I do that?"

Hannah rolled her eyes, again. "*You* wouldn't. But say you were in a fight and someone knifed you, here." She thrust a nonexistent blade into her stomach. "And you lost a whole pile of blood and they took you to the hospital and had to replace all the blood you lost. They would test your blood at the hospital before they gave you any new blood. Because, know what would happen if they gave you the wrong kind?" She leaned over the table and bared her vampire fangs at the kid.

"What?" He gulped and leaned back.

"You'd start to get little clumps, like those ones there, floating around inside you. And they'd get into all kinds of places they weren't supposed to and finally —" Hannah stopped and grabbed her throat. She made a choking sound. She opened her eyes wide and gasped, "You could die!"

She took her hands away and smiled. "That's why Count Kyle over here and I carry around this handy-dandy blood-typing kit. So we don't suck the wrong kind of blood!" She narrowed her eyes at the kid. "Hmm. What type of blood did you say this kid has?"

The kids looked at her warily and edged away. Kyle and Hannah broke out laughing.

"Hey, Mom, Kelly," Hannah said. "What do you think?"

"I think you should be thinking about a stage career, Hannah," Mom said.

She grinned. "Only if I don't make the WNBA. Want to try it?"

"You'll have to grow about two feet, first," I said. Hannah was the smallest kid on her basketball team, but that didn't stop her from being one of the top scorers. "Yeah, I'll try it," I said, sticking out my finger to Kyle.

"Don't trust me, Kel?" Hannah asked, all wide-eyed innocence.

"Not on your life." I knew Kyle wouldn't screw around. The two of us had an understanding. Kyle had been hanging with Hannah so long, he was practically a member of the family.

Kyle poked my finger and squeezed the blood onto slides. Hannah mixed the blue and yellow reagents with my blood and put them on the table.

"Now you, Mom," she said.

"I'll pass, Hannah."

"Aw, c'mon Mom." Hannah made her green eyes go all soft and liquidy. Limpid. That's what she did to her

12

eyes. She made them go limpid. "Dad and Caryn did it when they were here."

I had to hand it to my sister. She was good.

Mom looked at her. "Don't think I don't know what you're pulling. All right already. Stab me."

"Just a little prick, Mom," Hannah said happily, now that she had her way. "This is important information. Remember, sometimes what you don't know can hurt you."

"Neither of mine are getting specks in them," I said, slipping my samples under the microscope to double-check. "Nothing."

"That means you have type O blood," Kyle said. "You don't have either the A or B antigen."

"You too, Mom. Type O," Hannah said, checking the sample she'd taken from Mom. She looked again, and then put the slides under the microscope lens. "Type O it is. Most likely, that is," she mumbled, her forehead scrunched quizzically as she held our blood samples up to the light.

"Let me check it," said Kyle.

But Hannah nudged him away. She was a little pale all of a sudden. I didn't think anything of it at the time, but now, remembering how her voice sort of choked and the words came out all strangled, I can see that she was upset about something.

"I don't need a second opinion," she snapped at Kyle.

He shrugged. Mom started to take photos. The motor drive whirred, advancing the film frame after frame while Hannah and Kyle goofed off for the camera.

I had to admit the two of them had done a pretty good job. There was a big poster on one panel of the display called "Bloody Facts," along with a story about vampires. A chart explaining what blood types could be inherited from other blood types took up the middle panel, and their two-page written report was neatly tacked on the last panel. There was a stack of brochures on the table about blood donor clinics.

"Where did you get all this stuff?" Mom asked.

"We have connections," said Kyle. "My mom is a lab technologist at the hospital. She got us the reagent and showed us how to do the testing. My brother helped us with the computer graphics for the display."

Mom asked questions and took more pictures, while I waited impatiently. Kyle did most of the talking. Hannah stood beside him and glared silently. I figured she was ticked at him for hogging the spotlight. She didn't get to show off for Mom very often, either. After a few minutes I gave Mom a nudge.

"Great job, you guys," I said. "We have to go now, right, Mom?"

Mom's friend, Peter, met us at the restaurant, which sort of surprised me. I was a little disappointed at first that it wasn't just me and Mom after all, but I liked Peter and we had a good time.

I didn't find out what happened at the science fair after we left until Mom dropped me off at home later that night.

3

I heard Dad's voice before I even walked into the house.

"Answer me, Hannah."

His voice had that edge to it, the one it got when he was coming close to losing it. Which meant something awful had happened, because Dad's store of patience was huge. I could remember maybe twice in my entire life that he had ever lost his temper.

When Dad did lose it, we knew we were in real trouble. Hannah was definitely in deep. Trouble squared, by the sound of it.

I hung my coat in the closet, kicked most of the snow off my shoes and left them on the mat to dry. Then I did my best to sneak unobtrusively through the kitchen on the way to my room upstairs.

Hannah was sitting stone-faced at the table, staring hard at nothing. She was minus the wig and most of her make-up, but she was so pale that she looked more like a vampire than ever. Dad sat across from her, drumming the fingers of one hand on the table. Caryn sat between them, in my place; the place that used to be mine, that is. The grand inquisition was in progress.

"Never mind the cost of replacing the microscope, which you will find a way to pay for, by the way. Never mind all the work you and Kyle put into that project. Whatever possessed you to fight with your best friend?"

I snickered a little, making sure my face was turned away so Dad wouldn't see. Kyle and Hannah fighting was nothing new. Hannah had been bossing Kyle around and getting him into trouble since they were seven years old. Every once in a while he rebelled. They always made up. Even when we moved to a different neighborhood after Mom and Dad got divorced, the two of them stayed friends.

"It could have been a lot worse than a few stitches," Dad said.

Whoa. That got my attention. Stitches? I spoke before I stopped to think. "You actually hit him?" This *was* new.

"Butt out, Kelly." Hannah glared at me.

"That's enough, Hannah," Dad said. He shook his head at me. "Leave it alone, Kelly. This discussion doesn't involve you."

"Fine by me." I headed up the stairs to my room,

muttering. "Yes, thank you for asking. I had a perfectly lovely evening with Mother."

Actually, I was more than happy to stay out of the way. Seemed strange, though, that Caryn got to hang around. She and Dad weren't even married yet; she'd only been living with us for a few months. But the changes had started already. Big obvious changes like the renovations to our little galley kitchen for Caryn's catering business. The kitchen was now huge, with a stainless steel commercial fridge, two ovens, a pantry and specially designed drawers for organizing utensils.

It was a great kitchen, all right. Too great. Caryn was positively maniacal about keeping it clean. I sort of understood; it was her place of business. Hannah just avoided the kitchen altogether.

Other changes weren't so obvious, but for some reason they were almost harder to take. Like the way the sheets and towels smelled different because Caryn used a different laundry soap, or the way her chocolate sauce tasted sweeter than the stuff Mom made, or even the fact that their bedroom door was closed at night now, when Dad used to always leave it open.

I curled up with a book in my little alcove window seat. I could still hear the voices downstairs.

"Just tell me why you did this, Hannah, and maybe I can give the school some explanation for your behavior."

"We had an argument. No big deal."

"What were you arguing about? Not that that's any excuse."

There was silence. I couldn't hear Hannah's reply.

"Nothing? You were arguing about nothing? You

just up and punched your best friend about nothing?"

"I didn't punch him. I just sort of shoved him. He deserved it, showing off for his girlfriend. It's not my fault he tripped over a stupid chair and fell on the table."

Dad's voice was softer now. "Does it bother you that Kyle is dating someone?"

"Dad! Give me a break."

I didn't blame Hannah for being disgusted. As if anyone actually dated in grade eight.

"Shoving someone is physical violence, Hannah. Since when do you solve arguments with violence? Do you know Kyle could press charges against you?"

"He wouldn't do that. It was just a shove."

"Five stitches, Hannah. He had to get five stitches in his hand. How is he going to do his school work while the cuts heal?"

"Lucky him. He should be thanking me," Hannah shot back. Big mistake, I thought.

Dad's voice was hard and cold when he finally spoke again. "You don't seem to understand the seriousness of what you did."

"What do you want from me?!" Hannah was practically shouting now. "I'm sorry, okay? I'm sorry Kyle got hurt. I'm sorry I shoved him. I'm sorry he was being a jerk! I'm sorry we even did that stupid project!"

"I thought your project was tremendous." Dad sounded tired. I could barely make out what he was saying. "You're missing the point, Hannah. I think you'd better go to bed. It's late. We'll talk about this when we've both calmed down."

I could hear Hannah push her chair back and stomp up the stairs to the room beside mine. Bang! The door slammed. I stared out my window into the silence of the night, thinking that soon it would be warm enough to sit out on the roof again.

Hannah had made quite a scene, even for her. Not that I wasn't used to her dramatics. All her life she'd insisted on taking center stage. It was all I could do to keep from being dragged along with her.

She was barely five and I was eight when Mom and Dad's arguments started to be something more. We shared a room, then, in a different house. But sounds carried up to that room, too. At night, when their voices got loud, I would talk to Hannah to cover up the sound, to keep from being cast adrift inside my own body.

"What color do you think the wind is?" I asked one night.

Silence. Voices murmured below us in the kitchen.

"You can't see wind." Hannah was curled up in the corner of her bed against the wall, hugging her softest-ever. That's what she called the blanket Dad gave her as a "being born" present. Mine was a Pooh bear that I kept on my dresser. My bear had survived better than Hannah's softest-ever. The yellow satin blanket wasn't yellow anymore, except for the stitching which stood out against the faded fabric, and the wavy edges were tattered.

"Yes, you can," I told her. "You can see it moving through the trees, and you can see it making the grass bend."

Hannah considered this. "You can see it pushing against birds."

"And blowing away dandelion fluff."

"And blowing the leaves on the ground."

"Making waves in the water."

"The wind is blue when it's in the sky," Hannah decided. "Unless it's moving the clouds around, and then it's white."

"So when it's in the trees, it's green?" It was easy to follow her reasoning.

"Yeah, and when it's blowing in my hair, it's brown." She giggled and then stopped abruptly. More words, louder now, came from downstairs.

"I've had enough!" Mom's voice almost shrieked.

Hannah scrambled out of bed. "I'm going to stop them," she said, the color game forgotten.

"Hannah, stay here." Panic made my mouth dry and chalky tasting. "They're okay. They're just talking."

"No, they're not," she said, but she sat down on the edge of her bed. "Why are they talking so loud?"

"I don't know. Leave them alone. They won't get mad if we're good."

"They shouldn't talk so loud." She was moving again.

"Hannah!" I was pleading now, but it was too late. She was out the door. I crept to the top of the stairs and listened, huddled in the shadows against the wall.

Hannah marched down the stairs, stomped across the hall and threw open the swinging door into the kitchen. Bang!

"Stop it this minute!" she sobbed, louder than either of them. She hadn't been crying when she left our room. "I've had enough!" Big drama. Funny, too, turning their own words on them. Part of me admired her daring even then.

I held my breath. Couldn't believe it when Mom and Dad actually stopped fighting. They cuddled her, gave her something to drink, tucked her back in bed. I pretended to be sleeping the whole time, but I stayed awake, drifting inside myself most of the night, just in case.

All through the divorce, and all the time since, I'd stuck to my policy of staying out of everyone's way. It was safer. It was even comfortable. All I had to do was look at the sadness lingering in Dad's soft grey eyes for months after Mom left to know that I was right. If you got too close, you got hurt.

Hannah, though, wasn't the type to back off. All you had to do was watch her on the basketball court to know that. It was like she was possessed. I'd seen her dig an elbow into an opponent's ribs and be six steps away before the person knew what happened. Even in grade seven she made the senior team at her school. Now that she was in grade eight she was on the starting line-up and one of the top scorers. She spent hours practicing at the hoop that Dad put up for her over the garage.

Sometimes Hannah bugged people when she went too far, but the science fair was the first time she got into real trouble.

No one pressed any charges. Dad paid for the microscope that broke when Kyle fell on the table. He'd cut his hand on the broken glass. He and Hannah were disqualified, and Hannah was suspended for the last two days of the science fair. Plus she got a detention every day after school for a week so she missed her basketball practices and even a game.

Hannah was furious. She barely spoke to anyone at home the whole week. She stomped around the house glaring at us, especially at Dad, as if it was all his fault.

I think she must have met Natalie in detention. It was about then, anyway, that they started hanging around together. Kyle came by our place a few times, but Hannah refused to talk to him. After a while, he stopped showing up.

```
Class 8C, Mr. Cobol
Career and Life Management (C.A.L.M.)
In-Class Assign.#5: Write an imaginary obituary for yourself
```

Name _Hannah Farrell_ Date _March 11 98_ Class _8C_

Hannah Jayne Farrell - October 13, 2009

Passed away suddenly at the young age of 25, during a WNBA celebrity shoot out. The basket was good, but Hannah collapsed and died on the court.   **?**

Hannah was born on Nov. 25, 1985 (at least that's what she thought) in Black Diamond, AB. Despite a tragic childhood she became one of the world's best known celebrity athletes. She led her high school basketball team to the provincial championship and played college ball for the U of VIC Vikes when they won the CIAU Championship in 2005 and 2006. Hannah was named most valuable player and was recruited by the Houston Comets of the WNBA. She held the league's scoring title for a record-breaking three years in a row. At the time of her death, Hannah was the highest paid female athlete in history. She was struck down at the height of her career by a freak genetic heart disorder.

Hannah is survived by too many parents to name and one older sister. Thousands of fans mourn her passing. Memorial services will be held at the Hannah Farrell Gymnasium in Black Diamond. Cremation will follow and her ashes will be scattered during a private ceremony on her estate on Vancouver Island. **A- Well written! Lots of details. A truly tragic story!**

4

Dad and I ran together most mornings. He was the one who got me started running, a few years after Mom left. Neither of us was very good at talking; we ran.

I could tell he was bugged that week after the science fair because he ran harder and faster than usual, forgetting I was even there. He left me behind a couple of times and then jogged back with a sheepish grin on his face, shrugging an apology.

One morning when Dad was ahead of me, Sean suddenly appeared. It was almost like he'd been waiting for me. He actually changed direction, veered across the street and started running beside me.

"Hi!" he said. He wasn't even breathing hard.

I nodded to him, too surprised to answer.

"I've seen you running before. You must live around here."

I nodded again, to where Dad was jogging toward us, and finally found my tongue. "I run with my dad," I said briefly.

"Lucky," Sean said. "It would be a lot easier to get up some mornings if I had someone to run with."

I wasn't sure what exactly he meant by that, but he didn't seem to expect an answer. He kept talking without waiting for one. "The cross-country team could use some more people. Why don't you come out with us sometime? The coach was interested when I told him about you."

Now I *was* stunned. "You told the coach about me?"

"Yeah," Sean nodded. Then he must have noticed the expression on my face. "Shouldn't I have?"

I was saved from answering by Dad's return. I introduced them, Sean said "hi," and then nodded at both of us.

"This is my street. See you again." He turned at the corner, jogging backwards and waving. "Think about it, Kelly! You'd like it."

I was relieved when all Dad said was, "He seemed like a nice boy." He was obviously still preoccupied with Hannah, and for once, that was fine with me. I didn't know whether I was pleased or offended by Sean's invitation.

Hannah was so growly all week that I thought Dad might not take her on the ski trip we had planned for Sunday. I almost hoped she would have to stay home as part of her punishment. But Friday night Dad asked her if she was coming along.

"Who's going?" she wanted to know.

"Just the four of us," Dad said. "Unless you want to ask Kyle."

She looked like she wanted to say no. But the lure of the slopes must have been too much for her. "Yeah, okay," she muttered. "But I don't want to bring anybody."

We were up early Sunday so we could get to the hill before the lifts opened. Black Diamond, where we live, is on the prairies, but only about an hour from the mountains. A two-hour drive took us to some of the best skiing in the Rockies.

When we got to the hill, we unloaded all our gear and carried it up to the lodge, then bought lift tickets and went into the restaurant for breakfast.

"Where do you kidlets plan to ski?" Dad asked as he sipped his coffee and we waited for our orders.

"Dad," we groaned. One of these days, he was going to realize we weren't kidlets anymore.

"Sorry," he grinned, not at all sorry. "Where do you girls plan to ski? Or isn't it politically correct to call you girls, either?"

"It's better than kidlets," Caryn answered for us.

"Let's go right to the top and ski the bowl," Hannah said. "The snow is always better up there."

"Okay," Dad agreed. "But take at least one warm-up run first, and make sure you stay together."

My face must have shown my disappointment. Dad usually skied with us. I forgot that this was only Caryn's second time on a ski hill. She wasn't ready for the more difficult slopes yet.

"Caryn and I will meet you for lunch," Dad said. "Maybe we can all ski together this afternoon."

Hannah acted like she didn't care; she chewed her food and stared out the window. Dad and Caryn started talking about wedding plans. Every once in a while, one of them would ask Hannah or me what we thought, but it was obvious they were just trying to be polite. They weren't really interested in our opinions.

I tried to not let it bother me. I was looking forward to getting out on the slopes. "I hope Caryn is a fast learner so we can all ski together again," I said to Hannah as we were riding the chair lift up the mountain for our first run.

"Dream on. Even if we got to ski every weekend, which we don't, it would take her an entire season before she would be able to keep up with us. Dad will stay with her and we're stuck with each other."

"Thanks. I'm crazy about you, too. You could've asked Kyle to come along, you know."

"Kyle and I are not on speaking terms." Hannah stared straight ahead at the mountain. "Who cares anyway? I just want to ski."

When we got to the top, she lifted the safety bar on the chair and we slid off the lift and down the ramp. One of my boots was a little loose so I stopped to tighten the clips. When I looked up again, Hannah was gone.

I took my time. Hannah was going to have to wait for me at the bottom anyway. I don't know why she was always in such a hurry. But she always was, trying to squeeze in as many runs as she possibly could.

We first started to ski when Hannah was eight and I was eleven. Kyle usually came along on our day trips to Snow Valley. By our third or fourth trip we had conquered most of the intermediate slopes. Dad would wait at the top of a slope and watch us go down before following.

One day Hannah left all of us behind and took off down a side run. Kyle and I started to follow her. Suddenly the hill disappeared beneath me and I was airborne. I landed with a thump on the side of a mogul the size of a small house, turned on my skis and managed to get them pointed uphill so I could stop. I looked behind me in time to see Kyle lose an edge and topple sideways, limbs pointed in every direction.

Hannah was halfway down. I glanced at the run marker. It was a black diamond; she had taken off down an expert slope. Her skis were short enough that she could slide between the moguls, and that's what she was doing — darting in and out of the huge icy mounds and down the slope like she was born to it. My heart pounded in my chest and I held my breath, watching her, expecting her to miss a turn and splatter all over the hillside any minute. But she didn't.

When she got to the bottom of the run, she stopped and waved at us. She wanted us to follow her. Not me. I knew my limits. Kyle and I took off our skis and climbed back over the drop-off, then traversed the hill to get back on the right track. By now Dad had caught up.

Hannah was waiting for us at the bottom of the lift, breathless, with her face glowing. "Wow!" she said.

"Did you see me? I was good, wasn't I?"

Dad didn't think so. He placed one huge gloved hand on Hannah's shoulder and steered her into the lift line with him, leaving me to ride up with Kyle. When Hannah got off at the top, she was glowering. I could almost see the storm clouds rumbling in her eyes. We skied close together on the intermediate slopes the rest of the day.

But today I wasn't going to let Hannah spoil things for me. Skiing was best in the early morning before the slopes got crowded; I refused to be hurried. I was going to savor every minute. I slipped the slim pair of ski glasses that Caryn gave me for Christmas over my eyes. The contours of the slope jumped out at me through the yellow plastic. I pushed off, crossing the groomed run in long easy curves to get a feel for the slope and the rhythm of my own body.

It was easy to forget everything but the feel of the mountain rushing by. My skis swooshed quietly over the fresh snow, faster and faster. By the time I reached the end of the run I was skiing almost straight down, my skis parallel, my turns tight and quick, my heart racing. The breeze in my face changed to a cold, stinging blast. I took the last corner of the run and tucked against the wind, straightening and shifting my weight over the edge of my skis at the last minute to stop in a spray of snow.

Hannah was already in the lift line, waving at me. I ducked under the ropes to join her. The lift carried us higher, the sun rose over the mountain peaks behind us, sunshine suddenly spilled into the valley and onto the slopes. The soft, even light of early morning was transformed into an almost painful brilliance. I turned my face to the sun, felt its warm hands on my cheeks, breathed in the crisp, evergreen air.

A squirrel chattered at us as we passed through the tree tops. A white cascade tumbled to the ground as it scampered away. We continued higher up the mountain, moving through a silver glitter of ice crystals floating on the breath of morning. The entire scene was muffled, suspended in time.

"I feel like I'm inside one of those little glass snow-domes," I whispered.

I didn't realize I had said it out loud until Hannah murmured beside me. "Mmmm. Don't you wish we could stay up here forever?"

I turned to her in surprise. Her words were full of such longing. Her eyes were closed and her face lifted to the sun. "You can't beat a sunny day on a ski hill."

One run and Hannah was human again. I had to laugh. "Look at the mountain peaks." I suddenly forgave her, forgave Dad and Caryn, in a rush of exuberance that wanted to spill out like the sunshine around us. An eagle or hawk of some kind — I couldn't tell — was soaring above the mountain. "The mountains are so incredible. Nothing else seems like it could possibly have any significance next to them."

Hannah kept her eyes closed. "Mmm," she said again. "Almost."

I struggled to find the words for what I felt. "A day like this, a place like this, makes you feel more real and alive. It makes all the everyday stuff not matter one little bit."

"Like our father deserting us for another woman," Hannah said drily.

I shook my head, but didn't let go of my mood. "Can't you at least try to be fair, Hannah? I just mean things like . . . like having to do our own laundry."

That was Caryn's most recent decree. If we were going to change clothes three times a day, she said, we could do our own laundry. She'd marched us into the laundry room and demonstrated the proper use of the washing machine. At the time I was a little peeved. Now it seemed like it was too stupid to bother about.

"Like playing on a losing basketball team," Hannah added. Her team hadn't won a game yet this year.

"Like Peter showing up on my night with Mom."

"Like Kyle's stupid girlfriend." Hannah was getting into it now.

"Like Dad skiing with us for only half the day instead of the whole day."

"Like zits."

"Or my hat that doesn't match my ski jacket."

"Or having to use your big sister's hand-me-down skis." Hannah straightened her legs on the chair so the skis she was wearing, my old scratched pair, pointed to the sky.

Or whether Sean is interested in recruiting people for the cross-country team, or something else, I silently added to myself.

We were at the top again. This time Hannah waited until I was ready before she pointed her skis downhill and whooped, "Catch me if you can!"

We skied hard and fast all morning. We took face plants in the snow. Did spread eagles off the jumps built along the side of the runs. We laughed. We laughed so hard that we cried, happy to be alive on that day and in that place, where nothing mattered but the moment.

Whatever was bugging Hannah, she left it behind for those few hours.

Dad and Caryn felt it, too. We weren't quite as boisterous after they joined us, but by the middle of the afternoon we had Caryn going down the slalom course set up on one of the runs.

It was like a reprieve of some kind, I think now. The calm before the storm. It was the last ski trip we took that year. And the last time I remember feeling safe, feeling truly and gloriously alive, ecstatically alive, in a world that made sense. I sometimes wish, like Hannah, that we could have stayed on that mountain, at that time, forever.

5

Dad was a pipeline welder. After the divorce he worked mostly local jobs for oil and gas plants around Black Diamond so he could take care of Hannah and me. But in March, a few weeks after the science fair, he got a chance at a big-time welding job on a gas pipeline in northern B.C.

"Go," Caryn urged him. "I can handle things here until you get back. It's only for a few months."

I turned down the volume on the TV.

"I'm a little worried about Hannah," he said. "I don't know what's wrong with her lately. She's so sullen."

Caryn nodded. "I know. Teenagers can be awfully moody. Remember what it was like? Ecstatic one minute and sobbing your eyes out the next. Do you think it's something more than hormones?"

Dad shrugged. "I don't know what's going on. Kelly never acted like this."

"Maybe getting used to me is part of the problem," Caryn said. "Maybe this would be a good opportunity for us to get to know each other better."

"I would make a lot of money. Union rates." Dad was trying to talk himself into it. "We could take that vacation to Mexico next winter. A real honeymoon. What do you think, Kelly?"

Okay, so it was obvious that I was listening in on their conversation; it did concern me, after all. The thought of Dad going away, even for a few weeks, made my heart pound and my hands go cold and clammy. Which was ridiculous, I thought, swallowing the lump that rose in my throat. We were perfectly capable of looking after ourselves. This wasn't the first time Dad ever had to go out of town. But Caryn was here now.

I cleared my throat. "Could I get a new computer? A laptop?" I wasn't above being bribed.

Dad nodded. "No promises, but that's a definite possibility. A computer for you and Hannah."

"What do you mean you're going away? For how long?" Hannah demanded when Dad told her he was thinking about taking the job. "I don't want a stupid computer. You'll miss my basketball playoffs. Don't you have things to do to get ready for your wedding?"

"It's a small wedding, Hannah," Caryn said quietly. "You and Kelly can help me."

"Yeah, right."

"If you don't want a computer, maybe you want something else." I guess Dad figured that if a bribe worked on me it should work on Hannah, too.

"Oh, you mean like a father? A real father who actually lives with his kids instead of leaving them with some stranger?" Hannah was shouting. "Mom's already gone all the time. We hardly get to see her! Now you're going to dump us, too!"

She'd gone from zero to sixty in two seconds flat. Over what? Nothing. Dad was only going to be gone a couple of months, and he'd get some time off in between to come home. It turned out he was gone longer, but none of us knew that would happen at the time.

"I want a life! Mine sucks!" Hannah stomped upstairs. Her bedroom door slammed. Dad sighed and followed her.

"Hannah and I made a deal," he said when they came back down. He looked relieved and Hannah looked triumphant, even with her face blotchy red from crying. She sure knew how to pour it on when she wanted. "She's going to help out around here while I'm gone and I'm going to get her a CD player when I get back."

He turned to me. "And I'm going to call your mother and see if Hannah can spend Easter break with her. You, too, Kelly, if you'd like."

"Mom can come to my basketball tournament." Hannah could never let it go. "She'll love it."

"Okay," I said to Dad. I was pretty sure Mom was leaving on another photo shoot, but he'd find that out soon enough. He could be the one to tell Hannah.

Dad took the job. We spent the first weekend he was gone with Mom. It was the first Friday night I could remember in weeks that Hannah didn't go out.

I loved staying with Mom, especially since she converted half of her old loft apartment into a studio. Hannah and I used to bug her about getting a house so we could have our own rooms when we came over instead of having to share the sofa bed, but she would just say, "I'm not here enough to take care of it. This is all I need." Now I was glad she'd kept the apartment.

The vinegary smell from the darkroom filled the place, even the living area. Mom still liked to do her own developing, the old-fashioned way. The smell made my nostrils tingle. Photos of all sorts were plastered everywhere, some framed, some just tacked to the wall so that the edges curled.

My favorite photo was one of Hannah and me when we were little; Hannah was barely walking on chubby legs and I was about four or five, I guess. We were holding hands and walking down the sidewalk in front of our other house. Mom took the picture of us as we were walking away. It was one of the smaller ones, and stood in a frame on the bookshelf. It wasn't even in color, just black and white. What I liked about the photo was the way it was sharply in focus in the center and faded away to a blur around the edges.

"I don't understand your fascination with that photo," Mom said. "It's not really very good."

"I know," I said. It didn't matter that the photo wasn't an award winner. "I just like it, I guess. I like the way the edges fade and blur around us. That's how I feel sometimes. Blurry around the edges."

Hannah picked up the photo. "I hate how short and stubby and fat my legs look."

"You were a baby, sweetheart," Mom said.

"A fat baby. How come Kelly's not fat? Tell me that."

Meals at Mom's were usually pretty simple affairs. That night we made spaghetti — then indulged ourselves by leaving the dirty dishes in the sink and the splattered mess on the stove to clean up later — and played crokinole until the tips of our fingers got sore from flicking the wooden pieces.

Mom snapped about a hundred pictures of us that night; pictures of us tasting spaghetti, leaning over the crokinole board, sprawled on the floor cushions, kibitzing with each other; pictures of us eating popcorn, watching videos, crashed on the sofa, asleep. Sometimes she could go a little overboard trying to make up for the time she wasn't around.

I took some photos, too, mostly of Mom cooking spaghetti sauce, tasting the sauce from the spoon, and later, sitting down to the candlelit table and lifting her wine glass to us in a toast.

"What was I like as a baby?" Hannah asked Mom while we were making popcorn to eat while we watched a movie. "Was I fat when I was born, too?"

"You were chubby. You had a head of thick, dark hair like a gypsy. You came out hollering and you've never stopped," Mom teased.

"Mom! Be serious. Are you making all that up?"

"Well, you did cry for about six months straight.

I remember your father bringing you into my dark-room one day. 'I had to show you,' he said to me. 'Show me what?' I said. He brought you in to show me you'd stopped crying! We laughed so hard you started hollering again, and then we laughed even harder."

"Ha, ha," Hannah said. "No one seems to be laughing these days."

Mom and I ignored her and started talking about something else. Hannah's next words brought our conversation to a dead halt.

"I want to come live with you, Mom."

Mom let out her breath and put down the bowl of popcorn. She leaned against the counter. "Is something wrong at home? I thought you liked Caryn."

"Well, I don't. Not really. I can put up with her when Dad's around, but now he's not even there. He just left us with her, Mom. That's gotta be breaking the custody agreement in some way."

Mom smiled a little. "I doubt it."

Hannah looked at her feet and mumbled, "Anyway, I want to come live here."

She caught me totally off guard. When had she started thinking like that? She hadn't talked about living with Mom for years. I watched Mom carefully. I was pretty sure what her answer would be, which was why, even when I missed her so much it hurt to breathe, I never had the nerve to ask the question Hannah had just asked.

"Oh, Hannah. You know I adore you both. You know that, don't you?"

"Yeah, I know."

She looked at me. "Kelly?"

I nodded. "Sure, Mom. Of course we know that." Why does she need to hear us say it, I thought resentfully.

"It's not practical, Angel." Mom went over to Hannah and hugged her. "I'm not here enough. You need a family around you."

My stomach flip-flopped.

"You're my mother. You're family," said Hannah. She sounded as if she wasn't altogether sure.

"Yes," Mom said quietly. "But I'm also Maddie Farrell, photographer. And I need that, so much it scares me sometimes. Oh Hannah, I know I'm not a traditional mother. But I would completely lose who I am if I wasn't able to do what I do. I wouldn't be much good to anybody."

"Don't you even miss us? Doesn't it even bug you that someone else is taking care of us?" Hannah sniffed a little and wiped her eyes with her sleeve.

Mom sighed again and held Hannah close to her. "Of course I miss you. Of course it hurts every time I think about what I'm missing."

She stroked Hannah's hair. "I could apologize to you for so much, but I gave up trying to be someone I'm not. I'm comfortable with me, even if I'm not always comfortable with the choices I've made. And I'm eternally grateful that your father is who he is. Neither one of us can be everything you girls need, but between the two of us, I hope we do a decent enough job."

Hannah turned back to the counter and picked up

the dish of melted butter. She poured it over the popcorn. "Think what you want," she said quietly, wiping her eyes quickly one more time.

"Hannah, please try to understand."

"I understand. Never mind. It doesn't matter."

I turned away too, wiping the counter and putting away the popcorn maker to give myself time to stop shaking. It was pretty obvious that it did matter, but Hannah didn't want to talk about it anymore. I could've told her what Mom was going to say. I'd figured out a long time ago that Mom was the most exciting person in my life. I admired her and loved her fiercely. Part of me wanted to be like her. Dad, on the other hand, was there.

Hannah shrugged off the moment and Mom acted like it had never happened. On Saturday, Mom managed to catch half of Hannah's first basketball game before she had to go catch a plane to Israel for her next job.

After that it was just us — and Caryn. Caryn went all out. She watched all of Hannah's games, dragging me along to the last one, even though Hannah's team had been trounced the week before, and the game didn't mean anything.

Caryn took us out for pizza after, along with some of Hannah's friends. Not her basketball friends, but two other kids who had come out to watch her play. I'd never met Natalie or Lisa before. They weren't the same kids Hannah had hung around with the year before.

Kyle had come to the game with Amy. He introduced her to me when we were leaving. Caryn invited them to join us for pizza, but they had plans. I got the impression that Kyle didn't particularly like Natalie and Lisa.

I can't say I did, either. And I could see Caryn really didn't think much of the two of them lighting up a smoke at the pizza place.

"I don't know what your parents think of smoking," she said. "But I would much prefer you didn't smoke when you're out with us. Or visiting at our home, for that matter." Caryn, it was obvious, was out of her element; she would have been better off ignoring them.

"Sure," Natalie said. She took another drag and then butted out the cigarette. "No problem."

I watched Natalie and Hannah smirk at each other when Caryn wasn't looking. What a couple of brats, I thought.

All the same, if smoking a few cigarettes was all they were into, Caryn didn't have much to worry about. Even though Black Diamond was a city of over 50,000 it was still a pretty small town in a lot of ways. Everyone seemed to know everyone else. At least at school. People talked. I'd heard things about Natalie, and they weren't about what an upstanding citizen she was. I was even starting to hear things about Hannah.

Natalie, people said, liked to party. She knew where to get just about anything you wanted. Marijuana, hash, street pills, peelers, coke, anything. I didn't even know what peelers were. I didn't want to know.

I had a scary feeling that Hannah might, though.

I didn't want to know that, either. I was not my sister's keeper.

Hannah,

Outrageous. You were totally outrageous, my friend. Everyone is talking about it. How much did you drink!!? You just vanished. I couldn't find you anywhere and then next thing I know Kyle is dragging me into the bathroom and there you are. Out cold. Did you reek or what! Lisa is pissed. It took her all day to clean up the mess before her parents got home.

Your not mad are you? Kyle called the stepwitch. She completely blew a gasket. Hope you survived the explosion. This class is sooooo boring, I can't stand it. Meet me at the bricks at noon. I gotta know what happened.

Nat

6

Dad called often. I came close to telling him, one night, about Hannah's new friends. But what could he do? Besides, there was really nothing to tell. Hannah seemed to be making an effort to get along with Caryn. She actually cleaned her room.

One Friday shortly after Mom left for Israel, my friend Erin came over to watch videos. Hannah asked if she could spend the night at Natalie's place. At first it looked like Caryn was going to say no. "Why don't you invite her here instead?" she asked Hannah.

"Kelly and Erin will be here, for one thing," Hannah said. "Besides, Natalie's got a hot tub. Please?"

There was a long pause. "Okay," Caryn said finally. "As long as Natalie's parents are going to be home."

"They are," Hannah said. "You can call if you like."

Caryn did call. She also gave Hannah a ride over on her way to catering a dinner party.

The second the door closed behind them, Erin pounced on me. "Why didn't you tell me about Sean? Why do I have to find out from the gossip mongers?"

"There's nothing to tell," I said, surprised. "How do you know about it?"

"Don't give me that, Kelly Farrell. Sean asked you to join the cross-country team. Greg heard him tell the coach you were thinking about it, and he told Ashley of course, and then Ashley's whole group of gremlins descend on me wanting to know what's going on and I'm completely flabbergasted because my best friend hasn't said a word about it." Erin stopped for a breath.

"I never said I was thinking about it!" I was indignant. Who did Sean think he was?

"Don't change the subject."

"It wasn't a big deal, Erin," I said. "He just knows that I run, and the cross-country team needs runners. Period. End of story. I'm not interested."

"In the cross-country team or in Sean?"

"Neither. Are you satisfied?" Until then, I'd still been considering Sean's invitation. But I didn't need some guy putting words in my mouth, or the whole school thinking something was going on that wasn't. I'd put an end to it right now.

Erin snorted. "Not interested in Sean Erais. Not likely. I don't believe you. Let's see what you do when he invites you to the next dance."

Erin obviously knew something she wasn't telling.

"Now who's keeping secrets?"

She grinned. "Ashley told me he's going to call you."

I swallowed and tried not to let on that my heart had skipped a beat. "Well, when he does, *if* he does, I still won't be interested."

Erin shook her head. "You are in serious lack of a social life, my friend."

I looked at her pointedly until she sighed. "All right, already. Consider it dropped. But if he calls, you are to call me the next instant. Agreed?"

"Agreed." That's one of the reasons Erin's my best friend. She knows when to back off.

We were halfway through the movie when Caryn got home and collapsed on the sofa. It was a little after eleven. The phone rang less than thirty minutes later. "Maybe that's your dad," she said.

But when she picked up the phone and her face turned rigid and angry, I knew it wasn't.

She listened, scribbled something on a piece of paper, and then answered shortly, "I'll be right there."

"What's wrong?" I asked.

"That was Kyle. Seems your sister has had too much to drink at a party. She's sick."

"I thought Natalie's parents were home."

"They're not at Natalie's. Kyle gave me the address." She hesitated. "Kelly, would you come with me? I'm not sure what to say to her. And I'm furious."

Erin looked uncomfortable. I wished Caryn hadn't said anything in front of her. And I thought it was a little low, dragging me into it, but I didn't want to argue with Erin there. I guess I was worried about Hannah, too. "Yeah, okay."

We dropped Erin off at home on our way to get Hannah. I was glad we did when we discovered what was waiting for us. I wouldn't have wanted her to see it. I don't know what I was expecting, but it sure wasn't anything like what we found.

Caryn didn't have to worry about what to say to Hannah, because Hannah was way past being able to listen.

The house was wall-to-wall kids. I was almost scared to go in, and I'm pretty sure Caryn was, too. But she was angrier than she was scared, I guess, because she set her lips together tightly, kicked aside the muddy shoes littering the hallway and elbowed her way through the mob to where Kyle was waving at us.

Hannah was passed out in the bathtub. She was a mess. Covered in mud, her clothes wet. No socks or shoes; jeans rolled up at the ankles. There was mud on everything — the floor, the counter, the bathtub.

But worse than that, she had hurled all over the place. She was covered in the stuff. There were clumps of it in her hair. The bathroom reeked.

Hannah whimpered.

Caryn's face softened and she whispered, "Oh, Hannah. What have you done to yourself?"

I gagged and stumbled into the hallway for some fresh air. All I got was a lungful of cigarette smoke.

Then Caryn appeared and grabbed the nearest kid. "Do you live here?"

The kid pointed at a girl, Lisa. Caryn stalked over to

her. "I need a couple of blankets. Now."

Lisa nodded and scurried away. Caryn turned back to the bathroom. "I'm sorry, Kelly. I'm going to need your help." Her voice was shaking.

I nodded, gulped and followed her. The two of us cleaned Hannah up the best we could. She was shivering and shaking, and she kept moaning. "I'm so c-cold. I'm cold."

Caryn tried to wake her up, but Hannah was a dead weight, moaning, "I'm c-c-cold."

We managed to peel off her wet clothes. I found her pack in a corner and we got her into dry pyjamas. Lisa appeared with the blankets.

"What did she drink?" Caryn asked her. Lisa didn't know.

More quietly, but with a cutting edge in her voice, Caryn asked, "Did she take any drugs?"

Lisa shook her head. "No. No way."

"Are you sure?" Caryn stared at her. Lisa stepped back, turned and scuttled out of the room.

It took both of us to lift Hannah into a sitting position and get the blankets wrapped around her.

"Should I clean up in here?" I asked, looking at the pile of wet, dirty towels we'd left on the floor and the mud and vomit streaked all over the room.

"Leave it," Caryn said. "They can deal with it."

I held doors open while Caryn and Kyle carried Hannah to the car. People stared at us. The whole school was going to know what happened by Monday.

I wasn't much good to anyone after that, sitting outside the curtained-off little space in the emergency room. I looked straight ahead and tried to ignore the stares of nurses and other patients. Tried not to listen to Hannah screaming on the other side of the curtain, or to the doctor's curt, efficient questions.

When that proved impossible, I cut loose inside myself and drifted, let the words roll over me.

"No. Noo. Noooooooo! Get away!"

"It's okay. You're going to be just fine. Hold still now . . . What's her name?"

"Hannah. Hannah Farrell."

"Hold still, Hannah . . . Tuck that blanket a little tighter, will you, Wilma? Can you pull that overhead heater any closer? . . . You'll be fine. Let us get this needle in your arm now."

"Nooooo!"

"Hannah! That's enough. Wake up, Hannah. Give us some help here."

"BP ninety over sixty. Temperature thirty-four."

"Her veins keep collapsing. Get someone to help you hold her still. Let's try the other arm . . . Hannah! Hannah! Can you hear me? Snap out of it, now. You've got to hold still and let us help you."

"Go away. Go away! Go . . . a . . . waaaay!"

"Not yet, Hannah. We're not going anywhere. Let's try this one more time . . . You're her mother? Do you know how much she drank? Did she take anything else?"

"Nooooo! You're hurting me!"

"I don't know. The other kids at the party said there were no drugs, but . . . I don't know. I couldn't wake her up . . . she was so cold and wet."

"Stop it! It hurts! Noooo!"

"Hannah, that's enough! You're going to hurt a lot more if you don't let us help you. Okay, let's try it again."

"Is she going to be okay?"

"She'll be fine. Lucky for her she threw up. If we can ever get this IV in her — there. Finally. Okay now, Hannah. Take it easy. The hard part is over. You can sleep now."

Silence. The rustle of sheets.

"You can go home, Mrs. Farrell. She's just going to sleep the rest of the night. You can come back first thing in the morning and pick her up."

I heard the steely slide of the curtain being drawn back, and blinked at the doctor as he nodded at me and disappeared down the hall. Caryn and the nurse appeared in the hallway.

"There now, your daughter will be all right, Mrs. Farrell," said the nurse. "That's okay. A few tears will do you good. We've all been there."

No. We haven't all been there, I felt like saying. For some reason, I really hated that nurse.

"There's a dear," the nurse said, patting Caryn's hand.

I just wanted to get out of there. I wished Caryn hadn't asked me to help her. How did I end up in the middle of this? Why couldn't Hannah just've passed out and slept it off in some corner? She could've cleaned herself up the next day.

I was glad to get outside where I could breathe again. Caryn didn't say a word, except to ask me if I felt like driving home.

HANNAH,
   ARE YOU OKAY? I TRIED CALLING
AT HOME BUT CARYN# SAID
YOU WERE UNDER HOUSE ARREST.
I WISH YOU'D TALK TO ME!

   DON'T BE MAD PLEASE? I
DIDN'T KNOW WHAT ELSE TO DO.
I KNOW YOU GOT IN A PILE OF
TROUBLE, AND I'M SORRY, BUT
WHAT ELSE COULD I DO?

   I JUST WANT TO KNOW
WHY YOU'RE SO MAD AT ME.
IS IT BECAUSE OF AMY? IT'S
NOT LIKE YOU AND ME — WELL,
YOU KNOW. I WISH YOU'D GIVE
HER A CHANCE. WE COULD ALL
BE FRIENDS. YOU DON'T NEED
FRIENDS LIKE NATALIE AND LISA.

   TOO BAD THE TEAM STUNKSO
BAD IN THE TOURNAMENT. YOU
WERE GREAT THOUGH. YOU ALWAYS
ARE.
       FRIENDS?

            KYLE

7

I didn't sleep at all that night. Hannah gets plastered and has a nice nap on a comfy bed, while I lie awake all night, shaking. I bet Caryn didn't sleep either. We didn't say much to each other when we got home. We were both too exhausted.

Caryn was the one who grounded Hannah for the party episode. I'm not sure that it was such a good idea, but then, Mom was off in the Middle East somewhere and Dad wasn't going to be home again until the wedding.

If looks could kill, the look Hannah gave Caryn would have been the end of her. Amazingly, Caryn stared her down.

"There's nothing more to discuss, Hannah. I talked

to your father and we agreed. You mess up, you pay the price. Two weeks. You can rant and rave all you like, but in your own room, please. You can come out when you decide to be civil."

"What did you tell Ian?" she demanded.

"Since when do you call your father 'Ian'?"

Hannah ignored her. "What did you tell him?"

"I told him what happened."

"You had no right."

"Do you want to talk to him?" Caryn asked. "Call him. Tell him your side of the story. He's worried about you. We both are."

"Yeah, right," Hannah sneered. "That's why he's put a whole province between us. Forget it. I don't want to talk to him."

For the next two weeks, Caryn and Hannah circled each other like cats, and I kept firmly to my policy of staying out of the way.

I had to tell Erin what happened, of course. She sympathized, and even squelched some of the worst rumors at school. Sean didn't call; I didn't think he would and I didn't blame him. It was just as well. I avoided the other kids at school as much as possible and spent a lot of time in my darkroom.

Dad had built the darkroom and set me up with some secondhand equipment when I was about Hannah's age, after Mom bought me an expensive 35 mm camera — a Nikon — for Christmas. There were *some* advantages to having divorced parents.

I wanted to develop the photos I'd taken at Mom's. I'd already processed the film. The negatives were hanging there waiting to be turned into prints.

Hannah came into my darkroom one afternoon after school, when I was working on them. I guess she didn't have anything better to do. She sat on the only stool and watched while I dipped the exposed photographic paper into the tray of developer, swirled the solution gently as I kept an eye on the timer, then placed the developed print in the stopbath, fixed and washed it. The safe light made a soft red glow in the room.

I was pleased with the way the prints turned out, especially the one of Mom raising her wine glass. The photo caught the expression on her face I loved best. Her usually animated features and questioning eyes looked soft and settled, as if pausing to appreciate the moment, gather energy, before charging ahead again. I carefully hung the print up to dry.

"You look like that."

Hannah's voice startled me. I was wondering if I should develop the print a little more to deepen the shadows from the candlelight.

"You look like that," she repeated, "when you're reading, and especially when you're out on your roof hiding from the world."

"I don't hide. I just like the peace and quiet." But I smiled at Hannah's comment. The roof was the best part of the house we'd moved into after Mom and Dad split up. I was the oldest so I got to pick the bedroom I wanted. Hannah was spitting mad, but there was never any question. I took the corner room with the little alcove just large enough for a window seat. Huge double windows opened wide over a gently sloping roof. It was perfect. I could cosy into the corner to read by the window, or scramble out onto the cedar shakes and soak up the sun or the stars.

Dad didn't like me to be on the roof at first, but I took him out there one night when the sky was completely overwhelmed with stars. After that, he just warned me to be careful.

I looked at the photo of Mom again. "I look like that?"

"Yeah," Hannah said. "You look a lot like Mom, really. You have Dad's features but you look like Mom."

I did have a similar oval face with high cheekbones and a quizzical expression. Hannah has those cheekbones, too, but a fuller face, and darker complexion that sets off her dazzling green eyes. Mom's eyes. In the sunlight, copper highlights shimmer in her thick, dark brown hair. I have Dad's flecked grey eyes and his limp, light brown hair, cropped short. I'm plain and ordinary, while my sister has a sensuous, exotic look about her.

"I always thought you were the one who looked like Mom," I said. "You have her eyes." The red glow of the safe light softened Hannah's face. For once, she didn't look angry. She looked sort of sad.

"The rest of me doesn't look like anyone, though." She laughed, not a nice laugh. "I probably belong to the milkman."

I shrugged. I thought maybe I'd frame it and give it to Mom for her birthday.

There were times I wondered how Hannah and I could be sisters, but not because of our looks. We were different in other ways. Hannah was athletic and into team sports, which I couldn't stand.

I did like the high I got from running and the solitude of long, easy runs. I didn't need the cross-country team for that, and so I never considered joining. Until Sean brought it up. I signed up for the photo club because it gave me a chance to show my photos in public and learn techniques that Mom didn't have time to teach me.

I was a good student — at the top of my class. Hannah was smart enough, but she could care less about school. I liked to watch and listen, preferring the background. Hannah said what she was thinking, she drew people to her and thrived on the attention. I was planning on being a lawyer. Hannah didn't know what a plan was.

The biggest difference between us, though, was that Hannah wasn't scared of anything. Sometimes I felt like I was scared of everything.

What Hannah had done at the party scared me. I turned suddenly to face her. "Why did you drink so much?" The anger in my voice surprised me, but Hannah didn't flinch.

"It's not a big deal. Everyone does it. It's not like I meant to get sick and pass out. I was just celebrating with my buds."

"Celebrating what?"

Hannah gave this cocky smile and gestured carelessly with her hand. "You know. Being young and free. Life."

I could see I wasn't going to get a straight answer

out of her; she was hiding something. "Well, it's pretty tough to celebrate when you're out cold."

Hannah's smile disappeared and her voice turned hard. "We had a few drinks, okay? No one was driving. We were just talking and looking at the stars."

"Just a few drinks?" I raised my eyebrows at her. "Uh-huh. Sure."

"What is your problem? I didn't drink that much — I didn't even have a hangover. I don't know what all the fuss was about. Why'd she have to take me to the hospital? She always overreacts. Not that I'm surprised or anything. She lives to make me miserable."

I was thinking about the trouble that the doctor and nurse had getting the IV into Hannah's arm. More than twenty minutes, it took them. "Now who's overreacting?"

"It's true and you know it. She watches me like a hawk and jumps when I make the slightest twitch. Then I get to scurry back to my hole like a mouse."

I shrugged and turned back to my photos. I refused to take sides. Let the two of them duke it out. I had better things to do.

"As if Mom and Ian never got drunk when they were fourteen. As if you never drink." She was getting worked up now. "They just never catch you. They think you're so perfect, you'd never do anything like that."

"You're full of it and you know it. I've had a drink once or twice, but I'm not stupid enough to drink until I pass out. I didn't think you were either."

Hannah stood up, knocking over the stool. "Now you're taking her side."

"I am not."

"She's taking him away from us. Can't you see it?"

I didn't say anything. Because I felt that way too sometimes, even if I knew it wasn't quite true.

"No one listens to what I have to say. Ian doesn't care about what I want. He even brought her along to my birthday lunch, the one that's always been just him and me."

I mentally added her complaint to my list of all the changes that had happened since Caryn arrived on the scene. But I still thought Hannah was wrong about Dad. I changed the subject. "Why are you calling Dad 'Ian' all of a sudden?"

"It's his name, isn't it?" She was close to tears now. "Two weeks, Kelly! What am I going to do every night around this place? Ian's not home. Sure didn't take him long to run out on us. She doesn't really want me here — she's just trying to show me who's boss."

I kept my mouth shut. There was no way to win an argument with Hannah.

Hannah yanked the darkroom door open. "Yeah, well, she's not my boss — I don't care if I did screw up."

I couldn't help flinching when she slammed the door behind her. I tried to go back to developingprints, but I'd lost my concentration. The images refused to come to life on the paper. I cleaned up and went upstairs.

Hannah was crashed on the sofa in the family room. The TV was on, but she wasn't really watching. I hesitated. I thought about offering to call up the WNBA website on the Internet with her. But why should I set myself up for any more abuse?

I decided to go for a run instead. I didn't run as often with Dad being away, and suddenly I missed it. I was careful to run in the opposite direction from Sean's place.

I had better things to do, I thought, than babysit Hannah while she was grounded. I had homework; I didn't get good marks without working at it. And there was the dance at school Friday night. I didn't really want to go, but Erin would probably talk me into it.

Hannah didn't want or need me around anyway. Most of that week we barely spoke a word to each other.

Late Saturday, after midnight, I was reading in bed when Hannah came into my room. She was dressed to go out.

"Shhhh!" she whispered, her finger to her mouth. "Caryn's sleeping."

She grinned at me and crept quietly to my window. "See you later."

She didn't even ask me not to tell. She just left. I went to the window and watched her sneak quietly across the roof, grab onto the branch of the poplar that crowded close to the house, straddle the limb and shimmy down the tree to the top of the fence. She was gone. I had no idea what she planned on doing at one o'clock in the morning, but I was pretty sure it wasn't anything civic-minded.

I hated this. I couldn't tell on her without being a rat. She was my sister, after all. All I could do was go back to bed and refuse to worry. Hannah could take care of herself.

I read until my eyes burned, but even then I couldn't

sleep. I lay there in the dark, and eventually must have dozed off. I woke up when I heard Hannah stumble in through the window. She bumped into my bed and almost fell over. "Oops. Sorry," she giggled. "Shhhhh!"

She smelled rank. Booze, campfire and cigarette smoke. And something else, sweeter than tobacco smoke. Pot. I pulled the blankets over my head so I wouldn't cough.

8

Sunday afternoon, Kyle came by to see Hannah. Sundays are always lazy days at our place, and I was lounging on the big chair in the family room with a book when there was a knock at the back door.

"Hey, Kyle." I was glad to see him.

He followed me into the kitchen where Caryn was baking muffins for our school lunches.

"You're just in time to sample the first batch," Caryn said. "Here." She put two warm blueberry muffins on a plate for him. "I haven't thanked you properly yet for calling me from the party. I'm glad Hannah had someone looking out for her."

Kyle devoured a muffin in two bites. "Hannah wasn't too happy about it."

"She will be," Caryn assured him. "Give her time."

I left them talking and went upstairs to get Hannah. The shower was running so I knocked on the bathroom door. There was no answer. I knocked again and shouted, "Hey, Hannah!"

"What!"

"You've got company."

The shower stopped. "Who is it?" she called.

"Friend of yours." I evaded the question. "Hurry up!"

"Who?" she asked again, but I didn't answer.

Hannah came down a few minutes later in jeans and a baggy sweatshirt, sleeves pushed up over her elbows, rubbing a towel over her wet hair. She stopped on the stairs when she saw Kyle, and then scowled at me.

I couldn't help staring at her. Even after a shower, her face was pale and her eyes red and puffy. She pulled the sleeves of her sweatshirt down, but not before I saw an angry red burn on her arm.

"What are you doing here?" Hannah demanded.

Kyle stood up. "Are you all right?" He'd obviously noticed Hannah wasn't looking her best, too.

She ignored the question. "What are you doing here?"

"You won't talk to me at school."

"And you can't take a hint?"

Caryn interrupted. "Have a muffin, Hannah. Kelly and I will leave you two to talk."

"That's okay," Hannah said. "He's not staying."

Caryn left the room anyway, and I started to follow her.

"Stay, Kelly," Hannah said. I raised my eyebrows at the order. "Please," she added, although it was still more of an order than a request.

Kyle looked sort of pathetic, as if he wasn't sure whether he should stay or go. He glanced nervously at me and then started talking in a rush. "Hannah. Do you want me to break up with Amy? Because I will, you know. If it means you'll stop being so mad at me."

The hardness in Hannah's face melted and she gave Kyle this exasperated look. "Ohh, you're hopeless," she sighed. She sat down, picked up a muffin and began to peel the paper away. "No, you don't have to break up with Amy. What do I care if you want to make a fool of yourself?"

Kyle grinned at her. "So you'll hang out with us again and blow Natalie off? She's just a bully, if you ask me. She could care less about school."

"Nat's okay," Hannah said. The warning in her voice was clear. "Not everyone is into school, you know."

"Never mind school. It's what she is into that worries me. Her name should be Trouble."

I winced a little. Guys could be so dense. Didn't Kyle know when he'd won a round? Back off, Bozo, I wanted to say to him.

"You don't have to insult my friends." Hannah turned icy green eyes on him. She had an uncanny ability to make her eyes go from warm liquid to ice in a blink.

"Hannah, she's not your friend. Nat doesn't have friends. Nat has . . ." He struggled for a second, trying to come up with the right word. "Associates. Promise me you'll stay away from her."

"Don't tell me what to do, Kyle Tomas Hirano. It's

sure not going to do me much good to hang around home waiting for you to show up these days, is it?"

Kyle had the grace to let that one go. True, he hadn't been around much, but who would, with Hannah giving them the cold shoulder all the time?

"Why, Hannah? Why do you want to hang out with someone like Natalie?" He gave her a goofy grin. "Especially when you've got someone like me?"

Hannah didn't go for it though. She stared at him hard for a long time and then spoke quietly. "I'm not like you, Kyle. I'm not." She nodded in my direction. "You and Kelly are more alike. And, and . . . that Amy. I'm not ever going to get grades like you guys do, or be class president or even care about those things. I'm tired of people expecting me to be good at everything, just because Kelly is."

Now it was my fault. "Don't blame —"

She ignored me. Her voice was suddenly cold, matching her stare. "Maybe I'm more like Natalie than you know. Maybe I belong with someone like her."

She got up and left him sitting there.

"No, you don't," he answered quietly.

I tried to look sympathetic. "Do you want something to drink?" I asked him.

"No thanks," he said. "Guess I blew it, huh?"

I nodded.

"I'd better get going."

He looked so miserable I couldn't help but take pity on him. I walked him out. "Don't take it personally. She can't be civil to anyone these days."

I was surprised at how warm it was outside. The

snow was gone and there were currents of green rippling across the brown winter lawn.

Kyle picked up the basketball from the back porch and bounced it on the sidewalk. "Sometimes middle school really bites, you know. Everything changes so fast. I thought we'd always be friends."

"So what happened to you guys, anyway?" I asked, a little hesitantly.

"I don't know. I guess I've just been spending a lot of time with Amy this winter. I never thought it bothered her." He shook his head. "It doesn't make sense. I know I'm missing something . . . We did our science fair project together like always. Ever since she blew up at me that day, we've hardly spoken."

"How's your hand?"

He turned his palm up and spread his fingers. There was a fine white scar across his palm. "Just like new." He clenched it into a fist. "Did she tell you what happened?"

I shook my head.

"It happened so fast, I hardly knew myself. I was showing Amy everything, and getting ready to do her blood type for her. She wanted Hannah and me to do ours, too. I told her we'd done ours before, but she wanted us to do it again. I think she wanted to make sure it wasn't going to hurt or something.

"It wasn't a big deal, so I said, 'Sure.' Hannah didn't want to, though, and when I tried to talk her into it she got mad. Next thing I know she tells me to get out of her face and gives me a shove." Kyle suddenly stopped short and looked puzzled.

"And?" I prompted.

"That's it. Caught me totally by surprise," he finished, absently.

I nodded. Nobody seemed to have any idea what was going on in Hannah's head these days. "She's been doing that a lot lately. Losing her temper over nothing. Puberty, I guess." A feeble attempt at humor, but I was trying to make him feel better.

"Yeah, well, if that's what it is, then puberty sucks. She hardly talked to me after that, and since Lisa's party she's been avoiding me completely. I wouldn't even have gone, except I knew Hannah would be there and thought maybe I'd get a chance to talk to her."

"She was lucky you went. Caryn's right. Hannah doesn't even remember what happened at the hospital."

Kyle was holding the basketball, spinning it in his hands. "I was scared, Kelly. Natalie just laughed and told me to let her sleep it off. I didn't know what else to do except call."

I knew exactly how he felt. "I'd talk to her for you, but she doesn't exactly listen to me."

He nodded glumly and left, lifting one hand in a half-wave as he walked away.

I went upstairs, put on a sweater and crawled out my bedroom window onto the roof. I needed a break. There were only a few clouds gathering on the horizon, but I could smell fresh, clean rain on the way.

Hannah suddenly appeared beside me. "What did Kyle tell you?" she demanded.

"That he wants you and him to be friends again."

"He has a funny way of showing it, turning me in like that."

"Sounds like he didn't have much choice. Your *other* friends didn't seem to care too much."

Hannah stood up and started wandering along the peak of the roof. She picked up a handful of snow from a small patch tucked in behind the chimney and formed it into a snowball. "What did he tell you?"

"Don't worry. All he said was that he found you passed out. Nothing we didn't know already."

She threw the snowball against the fence in the back yard, almost losing her balance in the process. She made me nervous, walking along the roof like that. There were still slippery wet patches on the shakes. "Would you at least sit down."

She just laughed, and moved closer to the edge of the roof.

"Quit kidding around, Hannah."

She was walking along the edge now. "What's the matter, Kel? You're not worried about me too, are you? Now that would be a switch."

"Grow up," I told her.

"Don't you ever wonder why we're so different, Kel?" Her foot suddenly slipped and she leaned back toward the roof to keep her balance. "Well, don't you?"

"Not really," I answered nervously. "Come back here, Stupid."

"*I* do," she said. "I've been wondering a lot lately."

"C'mon, Hannah." I didn't know what she was getting at. "Sure we're different. You're more like

Mom, I'm more like Dad. So what?"

She was standing on the edge now with her back to me, staring out at the fields and prairie behind the alley. "This place is so depressing."

It *was* a bit of a mess this time of year, with all the snow melting and everything one big mud puddle. But from up here you could also see the snow-topped mountain peaks in the west standing out against the blue sky. I knew if we walked out on the prairie or down in the coulees, we'd find the first crocuses and tiny white moss phlox starting to bloom. In a few weeks, everything would turn green.

And soon, soon the birds would come back. Meadowlarks and robins, bluebirds, warblers, flickers, swallows, kingbirds. And the nighthawks. It was the nighthawks I loved to watch most from my perch on the roof, the nighthawks wheeling and diving through the sky like acrobats.

I didn't think it was depressing. The earth was just gathering itself, waiting for the right time to show what it could do.

Without warning, Hannah lifted her heels off the roof and stood on her toes, her arms straight out as if she was diving off the end of a platform. "One, two . . ." she counted.

My heart jumped into my throat and an icy chill stabbed right through me. "Hannah!" I choked. "Get back here. Now!"

Hannah froze. She stood poised at the edge.

Time stopped dead. In the sudden void I heard Hannah take one long ragged breath.

Then she put her arms down and stepped back. She turned silently, walked back along the roof and started climbing through the window, back into the house. Time jump-started with a jerk and stumbled forward again.

"That wasn't funny." I was suddenly furious. Who did she think she was? What gave her the right to mess with people like that?

"Butt out of my business, Kel. You can't handle the truth, anyway." Hannah disappeared.

My heartbeat slowly returned to normal. I stayed where I was until I was sure my knees would support me when I tried to get up. If Hannah wanted me to butt out, I could butt out. It was her life, after all. She could screw it up if she wanted to. Just as long as she didn't mess up mine too. I wasn't going to let her jerk me around.

That's what she was doing, wasn't it? Playing games. I couldn't imagine any other explanation.

Willow Park Middle School
1682 Park Ave. Black Diamond, Alberta T8M 5X6 ~ (403) 822-7854

April 30, 1998

Parents of: Hannah Farrell
              562 Willowglen Place
              Black Diamond, Alta T3P 8B2

Please be advised that Hannah has received a three-day in-
school suspension as a result of a verbal confrontation with
one of her teachers. Hannah's performance has seriously
deteriorated this semester, particularly in the past several
weeks. While we have spoken on several occasions with
respect to Hannah's attitude, her behavior has not improved.
I have attached a copy of the teacher's complaint to
underscore the seriousness of the situation, and would like
to meet with you as soon as possible. Please call my office
to arrange a convenient time.

Hannah's absences to date this semester are as follows:
Math, 11; Social Studies, 13; C.A.L.M., 4; Language Arts, 6;
Phys. Ed., 8; Guidance, 7; Home Ec., 8; and French, 15.

Hannah is more than capable of doing well in school, but her
continued absences and almost complete lack of interest in
class are seriously jeopardizing her ability to successfully
complete the eighth grade. Hopefully a joint effort
involving her parents and teachers will help put Hannah back
on track with her studies before it is too late.

Yours truly,

J. Potvin, Principal

JP/sg

Principal, J. Potvin

WILLOW PARK MIDDLE SCHOOL
INCIDENT REPORT

Date *April 29/98*

Student *HANNAH FARRELL* Grade *8*

Teacher *WHITLEY* Subject *SOCIAL ST.*

Specific Problem(s):
Constant talking back; rudeness. Persisently challenges my authority. Today's incident involved totally unacceptable language. I can't seem to get through to her and I simply cannot tolerate her behavior any longer. I would ask that she be removed from my class list as I am very close to overt and possibly inappropriate action - it's that bad! Please advise.

Achievement in subject to date:
Minimal. Has not completed an assignment in more than a month.

Action taken by teacher:

1) Dates of any discussions with student *Almost daily*

Results: *with no improvement*

2) Dates of phone calls to parents *various*

Results: *No change*

3) Other: *Numerous detentions*

Administrator's Response:
In school suspension & transfer to another class. Parent Interview requested

[illegible] — Administrator's Signature

M Whitley — Teacher's Signature

9

Not all of the trouble Hannah got into was totally her fault. I had some of the same teachers when I was in junior high school, before they changed it to middle school, and there were a couple of total lost causes.

Mrs. Whitley, the Social Studies teacher, was definitely one of the more severe cases. I actually felt sorry for her. Whitley used to fall apart regularly, at least once a week or so, about nothing. She had nerves of gossamer. We would all be sitting there, minding our own business, doing our maps or working on reports and next thing we knew, Whitless was sniffling. She'd excuse herself and the class would turn into a free-for-all until the bell.

Sometimes it happened if one of us students argued

with her about an answer, or drew a particularly nasty picture on the board. Mostly it happened for no reason at all. We laughed, but it also embarrassed us. When she turned out to be one of Hannah's grade eight teachers, I was surprised to find out she was still teaching.

Then there was Mr. Bergen. Mathematics. This was a guy who wore plaid polyester pants to school. You could tell what he'd had for lunch by looking at his tie. How were we supposed to respect that? He was more interested in telling us what a great fisherman he was or how his son was going to be a brilliant scientist, than he was in teaching us how to multiply fractions. That was okay by most of the class, mind you. It's just that he was such a joke as a teacher.

I survived because I read the textbook and for the most part, taught myself. I could see Hannah having trouble handling it, though. She'd never be able to resist thinking up ways to make Mrs. Whitley cry or to get Mr. Bergen going on a fish story and see how long she could keep him at it. After a while, it wouldn't even be a challenge for her. She'd get bored and skip class. Which is what she did, I guess.

There were some great teachers too, of course. Mr. Cobal taught C.A.L.M. He didn't get all tied in a knot every time someone disagreed with him. He encouraged it, as long as you could back up your argument with good reasons. The Language Arts teacher, Mrs. Rogalsky, was okay too. She came up with some interesting assignments.

When the letter arrived from the school, Caryn made herself a cup of tea and sat at the kitchen table for a long time. I felt a little sorry for her — I could see she didn't know what to do. So she waited for Dad. He was home a week later.

Dad's face got all rigid when Caryn showed him the letter. He called the school to set up an appointment and then grounded Hannah. It wouldn't have been so bad if he'd just said, "You're grounded," and that had been the end of it. But he went on.

"Look, Hannah," Dad said. "I know it's tough for you right now, but you have to get it together and put in some effort at school. You'll have the entire summer to goof off."

Hannah didn't bother to reply. Sitting at the dining room table with my homework spread out in front of me, I could see her stony face. It was a face she wore a lot these days. It made her look hard 'round the edges, like nothing was going to penetrate. She was staring at the surface of the kitchen table and running her fingernail back and forth along the edge.

"Talk to me," Dad said. He reached across the table and held Hannah's hands in his own. "What is the problem?"

Hannah pulled her hands away. "I don't have a problem. My teachers are dorks. What does the letter say?"

"I don't want to hear you talk about your teachers like that." Dad picked up the letter. He was careful not to let her see it; it was obvious there was something he didn't want her to read. "According to this, you have missed more than fifty classes in four months."

"They're just doing this to cover up what lousy teachers they are. I haven't missed that many classes.

Mostly only because of dentist or doctor's appointments. Lots of times I'm just a few minutes late and they mark me absent and then don't change it."

"Why are you a few minutes late in the first place?" Caryn asked. Hannah glared at her from under the hair hanging in front of her face and didn't say a word. I could almost hear her thinking, *Get out of my face. This is none of your business.*

Dad sighed. "Caryn is the one who gets the calls from the school when I'm not home, you know. Now tell me what's going on."

"I told you. Nothing. I had to hand in this assignment, but I couldn't find the teacher anywhere, so I was late. Period. Mrs. Whitley is the one who went ballistic." Hannah mimicked her teacher. 'You're not anything like your sister,' she says. You don't expect me to take that, do you? She's always doing that, comparing me to Kelly."

"The year is more than half over," Dad said. "If you've been having problems, why didn't you talk to us about your teachers before?"

Hannah looked at him then. No, she threw daggers at him with her eyes. "I believe I did, Ian. You said to give it time. Remember?"

"No, I don't."

Dad sounded so helpless. I didn't understand why Hannah was treating him like this. Like she was trying to hurt him. Why couldn't the two of them talk without fighting anymore? He paused before adding quietly, "Mr. Potvin implied over the phone that you were drinking. Were you?"

"No."

"Then where would he get that idea?"

"So call me a liar. No one listens to me anyway."

"I'm not calling you a liar. But I have a hard time believing your teachers are out to get you."

Hannah stared at the table again. "Whatever."

"I've had about enough, Hannah," Dad said. "Until we meet with your principal and find out what's happening, you are grounded. Straight home after school, understand?"

"But I told you what's happening!"

"We'd like to hear the school's version, too."

"So you're grounding me."

"I believe that's what I said. You can use the time to catch up on your homework assignments. And from now on, we'll make your appointments for after school."

"But I play basketball after school!"

Dad thought a bit. He might have glanced at Caryn. I couldn't see . . .

"The season is over, isn't it?" Caryn said quietly. She was right. Hannah's team hadn't even come close to making the playoffs.

"Yeah. But we still get together and play."

"Well, not for the next few days you don't," Dad said. "And I suspect if things don't improve in school, you won't be playing basketball at all next season."

"You can't do that!" Hannah shouted.

"I'm not doing anything — yet!" Dad's voice was getting pretty loud, too. "But I certainly can if I decide that it will get your attention. It may not be up to us.

The school may decide you can't play. Did you ever think of that?"

"They can't cut me from the team as long as I'm passing."

"Well, that's what this is all about, isn't it? How are you going to pass if you don't even show up for class? You've got to start realizing that your behavior has consequences."

Hannah shoved her chair back from the table and got up. She walked up the stairs stiffly, pausing at the top to turn back and say, "Thanks so much for believing me. It's nice to know you'll take the word of a teacher, *Father*, before the word of your own *daughter*." She slammed her bedroom door.

After she'd gone, Dad lost it for a few minutes, actually tore up the letter from the school and tossed the pieces into the garbage. He looked at Caryn, bewildered. "I don't know what's wrong with her!" Then he took a beer out of the fridge and sat at the kitchen table. Caryn went over to him and massaged his shoulders.

"I didn't expect it to be like this while you were gone," she said. "I don't know how to deal with her."

Dad reached up and held her hand.

And I resented them all. Hannah for making so much trouble. The teacher for comparing Hannah to me. Dad for not sticking up for Hannah. Caryn for making it sound like Hannah was something that could be slotted into some sort of in-basket to be "dealt" with. Dad and Caryn for just being there together while Hannah was upstairs, alone, and I was sitting in the other room. Alone.

The phone rang. I picked it up, grateful for the interruption. The last thing I expected was to hear Sean's voice on the other end.

"Hi, Kelly. This is Sean."

"Oh, hi, Sean."

"Did I call at a bad time?"

I cleared my throat and tried to sound less like an idiot. "No. It's okay."

"I haven't seen you running lately. The team started outdoor training a while back, and when you didn't show, I thought, well, it's not too late to join. We could really use you on the team."

"Thanks, Sean." I was determined to be polite but firm. "Really. I appreciate you thinking of me and everything, but I'm just not interested. I'm busy enough with school and the photo club."

"You're a photographer? I didn't know that. Maybe sometime you could show me your photos."

The idea of Sean coming to my house, with Hannah the way she was lately, made me cringe. "Maybe," I said, as vaguely as I could.

"Look. You could just come out to one or two practices, get a feel for what it's like."

"I don't think so."

A sigh came over the line. "Well, okay. If that's the way you want it. If you change your mind, call me. There's always the fall season."

I felt a tinge of regret as I hung up. But at least there was one less complication in my life.

Hannah refused to come down for dinner. Caryn

heated a plate of leftovers and asked me to take it up to her.

"Hey." I knocked on her door. "Are you hungry?"

There was no response. I opened the door a bit and stuck my head in. Hannah was sprawled across her bed, her face buried in her pillow. Her softest-ever was lying in a heap in the corner. I put the plate on her dresser, then picked up the blanket and tucked it around her.

"Get out of my room," Hannah said. "And take this rag with you! I don't want it." She threw the blanket at me. I caught it.

"I'm going," I said. "I just brought you something to eat."

She sat up. One side of her face had angry red marks on it from her quilt. "You could have stuck up for me."

"Geez, Hannah. You told me to butt out, remember? Why don't you just apologize for screwing up? Then no one would yell and you wouldn't get in half as much trouble."

"I didn't screw up. You know how Whitless is. You could have told them."

"Yeah, I know," I sighed. "Look, I'm sorry she expects you to be like me. That's not fair. But it's not my fault. And you still skipped classes. You must have done something to set her off."

"Aw, forget it. Get out of my life. If you don't mind."

Now I was fuming. "I wish I could! All we do anymore is tiptoe around you!" I slammed her door as I left and stomped into my own room, slamming that door too. I knew I was the one being childish now, but I couldn't help it.

I felt like tossing Hannah's precious softest-ever out the window. She obviously didn't want it anymore. I threw it into the corner of my closet.

I never knew how the meeting with the principal turned out, but Hannah was back in class after three days and there wasn't any more trouble, for a while at least. We were all too busy getting ready for Dad and Caryn's wedding to pay much attention to her.

In turn, she ignored all the wedding activity. She dug out our photo albums and spent hours staring at our baby pictures, as if she could make those days come back by wishing hard enough.

How are you my loves —

The photo shoot in Ekron went well. It is amazing stuff the archeologists are discovering. Did you know the Philistines captured the ark and then gave it back because of the bad luck it brought? Peter and I are enjoying a short holiday in the southern part of Spain. Costa del Sol area. It is wonderfully hot. We're surrounded by all the famous monuments like Granada, the Alhambra, Cordoba, Mesquita, Sevilla, etc. You'd love it! Wish you were here! Another assignment in Belfast next, and then home. Wish your Dad all the best from me on the happy occasion.

See you soon,
Mum

PS. Photo on front is the condo where we're staying—very nice!

Kelly and Hannah Farrell
562 Willowglen Place
Black Diamond, Alberta
T3P 8B2
CANADA

Puente Romano Hotel, Marbella
© STUDIO MARBELLA
Fotografía: Peio Aacarte
Distribuye: STUDIO MARBELLA - Tel: (95) 323 76 58

10

The actual wedding day was kind of anticlimactic as far as I was concerned. I mean, Caryn had been living with us for close to six months already. The reception was at our place, and I retreated to the roof as soon I could decently disappear. I needed to get away from the commotion. Besides, Hannah was being loud, rude and obnoxious. And for some obscure reason, Dad was letting her get away with it. Maybe he was too happy to notice at first. But she managed to get his attention eventually.

"Let's see how many famous stepmothers we can name." Hannah's voice carried through the entire room. I froze with a bowl of shrimp in my hands. People sort of chuckled. Mostly, they were family and a few friends. It was a small wedding and an informal reception. More of a party, really.

"I'll start," Hannah said. "Cinderella's stepmother."

Caryn laughed. "Snow White had a stepmother."

Okay, I thought, relaxing a little. Caryn's going to be a sport about it. She should be.

"Claudius was Hamlet's stepfather," said someone else. "And there was a stepmother in one of Shakespeare's other plays. *Cymbeline*, I think."

"I bet all of them were wicked, weren't they?" Hannah's voice got louder. "Why do you think that is? Where do you think the word stepmother came from, anyway?"

Before anyone could utter a word, Hannah answered herself.

"I think stepmothers and stepfathers are called that because they are a step below the real thing."

Caryn's brother Steve almost choked on his stuffed mushroom and the rest of the room got awful quiet, awful fast. Granny flushed, cleared her throat, then turned to Caryn and asked her what was happening in the catering business. Dad took Hannah by the arm and steered her out of the room.

"You and I are going to have a chat," he said quietly.

"What?" Hannah muttered. "It was just a joke!"

That's when I excused myself and climbed out onto the roof. The sun was low in the west. The evening air was beginning to cool and the sky was softening into a dusky blue. Long shadows groped across the river valley into the city. Here and there, house lights flicked on. A thin line glimmered at the end of the field where the sun reflected off a small pond.

Spread out before me, the evening was perfectly still, like God had pushed pause. And then I heard the nighthawks. The familiar, vibrating buzz.

My eyes searched the sky and finally found them. Beyond the lights, above the field behind our house, two, no, three birds climbed in steep spirals. Their long pointed wings beat slow and powerful, then suddenly erratic and frantic. The birds gyrated wildly upward. A harsh, piercing call punctuated their climb.

"Welcome back," I whispered. I suppose the fact that the nighthawks returned on the day Dad and Caryn were married could be seen as symbolic of something, but it wasn't that much of a coincidence when you think about it. The wedding was in spring, when migratory birds return to their breeding ground. Not much to wonder at in that.

A tiny thrill shivered through me and raised goosebumps on my bare arms as I watched the birds perform. At first they looked awkward, jerking around all over the place like crazy things. They circled higher and higher, until I almost lost the dark tiny flecks in the failing light.

Then one fleck stopped, poised above the world. And dove. The nighthawk fell like a stone. My heart was pounding.

I watched it hurtle closer and closer to the earth. It passed through the clear heights, then dissolved into the shadows. I held my breath, heard the quivering hum of wind sing through its wings, the vibrating buzz accelerate into a swooping crescendo. And then end.

Bursting out of the shadows, the nighthawk arced skyward.

A second crescendo buzzed further out, and then a third, softened by distance. Three forms began another wild, gyrating climb into the dying light. I went with them.

Over and over again, we climbed high into the sky and then dove back to earth. We were still flying when the sun disappeared and the remains of the day turned flat and ashen.

"May I join you?" Caryn poked her head out my window.

"If you want." It's not that I didn't like Caryn. She was okay for the most part. When she didn't try too hard. I'd pretty much figured out by then that Mom and Dad were permanent history, a concept Hannah still seemed to have trouble grasping.

Caryn hitched her dress up and crawled through the window. She didn't come all the way out, but sat on the broad sill with her stocking feet resting on the shakes, elbows on her knees. Hannah would sit like that, I thought.

"You're going to snag your pantyhose," I warned.

She shrugged. "I'm too tired to care."

Neither of us said anything for a long time. We watched those crazy birds diving through the sky. Somehow they made the world seem less mixed up.

Mom was in Spain with Peter. No, they had probably moved on by now, to the job in Belfast she'd written about in her postcard. I was used to getting postcards and birthday cards from around the world.

They were all pretty much the same. In every one Mom wrote about how she missed us and how incredible the country was and how one day she was going to take us with her to see that part of the world.

Maybe she would, too. One day.

But today Dad had married someone else. I suppose I was happy for him, that he had someone. For now. For however long it lasted. She was sitting beside me on the roof. She didn't own a camera or even know what an aperture was. She ran a small catering business out of our home — her home now, too. She was there and Mom wasn't.

I didn't have a choice in the matter, so I might as well make the best of it. As long as Caryn didn't think she was going to be my buddy.

Caryn's voice broke into my thoughts. "Do you know what kind of birds they are?"

"Nighthawks," I murmured. "They come out at dusk."

Caryn nodded silently.

How could life lose its equilibrium so quickly? Where did Hannah and I fit into this new arrangement? Knowing it was coming hadn't prepared me for the reality. Suddenly Caryn had all the power. She was in charge, just when Hannah and I were getting used to taking care of the house, and Dad, and ourselves.

It wasn't too bad for me. I only had another year of high school and then I'd be off to university and out on my own. Hannah was going to be home for another four or five years. I suddenly understood why she'd asked Mom about living with her.

Sitting on the roof, surrounded by soft grey dusk, everything seemed safe and peaceful, the reality of the day far off. Without really stopping to think, I said, "Hannah didn't mean it."

"Yes, she did," Caryn answered flatly. She looked out at the horizon and smiled a little. "It's her way of making sure I understand my place."

I thought about that and nodded. "Yeah, I guess. But I think it's also because she doesn't understand *her* place. Having a stepmother is . . ." I fumbled a bit, squirming. This conversation was going too far too quickly for me. "Well, a little weird."

"*Being* a stepmother is a little weird, too."

I was shocked into silence. Caryn sounded angry. Okay, so things weren't all that easy for her, either. She didn't have to tell me. I didn't want to know. I kept focused on the birds in the distance. But out of the corner of one eye I saw a movement in the room behind us. Hannah was standing there in the dark.

After a long uncomfortable silence, as if she wasn't sure what to say either, Caryn spoke again. "I'm sorry. You and Hannah come with the territory," she said.

My face must have shown my confusion. Caryn shook her head and laughed — a funny kind of dry laugh. I got the feeling she was laughing at herself. "I guess I got that wrong, too. I am so bad at this stuff. Let me try again." She took a deep breath. "What I meant was, I chose your dad, which meant I chose you and Hannah as well. You are both part of who he is. There was never any question of loving him, without loving you. Without you, he'd be a different person;

I may not even have loved that other Ian." She shook her head. "Oh God, now I'm confused. It's been quite a day."

"That's okay," I said. "I know what you mean." At the time I didn't have a clue, but I sure wanted Caryn to quit talking about it. It wasn't until later that I realized she was trying to reassure me that Hannah and I were not just excess baggage, that we had a place in the life she and Dad were making.

I tried to catch a glimpse of Hannah, but she was gone. Caryn and I watched the birds. They seemed so perfectly in tune with their world, I envied them. And somehow, the way the nighthawks flew, always the same, always pulling out of their dives, was enough to bring all the loose pieces and dangling ends of my own world together to make some kind of sense.

"Why do they fly like that?" Caryn asked.

I shrugged. "I don't know." I'd wondered about it, too. I thought maybe it had something to do with their mating rituals. Except I knew from watching them the year before that they flew like that for most of the summer, not just in the spring.

"A good bird book would probably tell you."

"Yeah, probably."

Caryn sighed. "This is nice. I needed a break from all the fuss downstairs. But I guess I better get back to the clan."

I nodded. Caryn managed to swing her legs back into the house until she was sitting side-saddle on the window sill. "Thanks for sharing your piece of the sky. When you're finished watching the nighthawks, there's still a lot of food downstairs. Even Hannah and my glutton of a brother can't devour it all." She ducked through the open window and was gone.

I turned my attention back to the birds. When night surrounded me and I could no longer see them, I could still hear them calling as they climbed between the stars.

I was just going to head back to the party downstairs, when Hannah appeared at the window in jeans and a sweatshirt, carrying her jacket. She looked at me and then down the alley. A set of car headlights blinked on and off at the end of the block.

"This is really why you'd like to have my room — so you could sneak out easier," I said. "Isn't it?"

"Don't you dare say a word," Hannah said. "I told them I was tired and was going to bed." She walked along the roof to the edge.

"Who do you know old enough to drive?" None of Hannah's friends that I knew were old enough to have a licence.

She looked back at me. "Just some kids. Lisa and Natalie are going too. I know what I'm doing."

"And what exactly is that?"

"Geez, Kelly. You sound like Dad. We're just going to hang out in the park. No big deal."

A nighthawk picked that moment to buzz-dive over Hannah's head. She didn't flinch. "Whoa. Was that a bat?"

"Nighthawk. There's three of them out there."

Hannah lifted one eyebrow at me. "Cool. Speed demons, eh?"

"I guess." When she said that, called the nighthawks speed demons, it seemed to change them into something else. Suddenly their dives seemed desperate, reckless. Defiant.

"Look, Kelly. You won't say anything, will you? They're so wrapped up in each other, they'll never notice. I'll probably be back before people leave. I'm just getting out of their way."

I sighed. "It is their wedding day, Hannah. They're supposed to be wrapped up in each other."

"I know it." Hannah sounded older than fourteen. "Doesn't mean I have to like it."

"I won't say anything. It's your skin if they find out."

"Yeah," she grinned. "But what they don't know can't hurt me." She grabbed a tree branch, swung herself through empty air onto a lower branch and was gone.

The last thing I did that night, after congratulating Dad and Caryn one last time, was check my dictionary. *Step — (pref), denoting nominal relationship similar to one specified, resulting from remarriage of a parent*. That wasn't much help. I looked up nominal. *Existing in name only, not real or actual; virtually nothing, much below actual value of thing.*

I didn't think I would tell Hannah that Caryn existed in name only, as far as being a parent was concerned. Dictionary definitions were useless most of the time anyway. I was beginning to figure out that a word on its own didn't mean much. Most of what a word meant depended on who was using it. Hannah's nighthawk and my nighthawk were two completely different things.

Hannah would have loved the dictionary's definition, though. Her own version wasn't that far off. She wouldn't have stopped to think that if a step*mother* was virtually nothing, then so was a step*daughter*.

I didn't hear Hannah come in. But I did hear her sometime early in the morning, throwing up in the bathroom across the hall.

On saturday night I lost my girl,
and where do you think I found her?
up on the moon singing a tune,
with all the stars around her.

11

If I'd been the one arrested, I would've died.

As it was, I almost passed out when I opened the door and two police officers were standing there. They filled the doorway.

"Good morning. Is Hannah Farrell home, please?" They were so polite it was scary.

The words echoed in my ears, which were already ringing from all the blood rushing out of my head. "Uh, sorry. No. She's not," I said.

"How about your parents?"

Caryn came around the corner, wearing jeans and an old shirt of Dad's with paint smears all over it, wiping her hands on a rag. She'd been in the back yard painting the deck chairs. Not exactly a great first impression to make when you have two police officers standing in your doorway. But it didn't seem to faze her.

"Hello," she said. "Can I help you?"

"We're looking for Hannah, Mrs. Farrell."

It sounded funny to hear Caryn called that. It was more than a month since the wedding, but I still wasn't used to it.

"We'd like to ask her some questions. Is she home?"

Didn't I already tell them she wasn't?

Caryn spoke in clipped sentences. "I'm sorry. She stayed at a friend's last night. We expect her home shortly."

"Perhaps we could ask you to bring her down to the station when she gets back."

Caryn sighed. "I think you'd better talk to Hannah's father. He's out back. I'll get him."

She invited them inside and left to get Dad. There I was, standing in the front entrance with two cops. I wasn't sure how to make my escape.

"May we sit down?" one of them asked.

"Sure," I gulped. I showed them into the living room. The occasion seemed to call for something more formal than the kitchen table. As soon as Dad and Caryn came back, I was gone. Not far, though. I sat at the top of the stairs, holding onto the oak railing, shaking.

"I'm Ian Farrell, Hannah's father," Dad said. "Is there something I can do for you officers?"

"Constable Vanderwahl and Constable Tiegan," said one of the cops. "If you don't mind, we'd like to ask Hannah some questions."

I got the feeling it didn't matter a whole lot if

anyone minded or not. I had to give Dad credit. He didn't miss a beat. My palms were cold and clammy. I couldn't stop shaking.

"Something I should know about?" he asked.

"We have information to the effect that your daughter was one of several youths involved in a break-and-enter incident recently."

"What kind of information?"

"Someone saw her, sir."

There was a pause. "What exactly happened?"

"Several youths gained entry to a private residence through an unsecured window. They took a quantity of liquor and cigarettes, a CD player and a VCR."

I bet Dad was wishing he was back in B.C. They'd been getting heavy rains at the job site for the past week and everyone had been sent home until the weather cleared and the site dried out some.

The silence lasted until one of the officers finally cleared his throat. "Would you mind bringing her down to the station when she gets home, sir? If not, we'll come back and pick her up later."

"I'll bring her down."

"Thank you, sir."

I snuck into my room and sat on the bed until the shaking finally stopped. All I could think about was that I didn't want to be anywhere in the neighborhood when Hannah came home. The tension had already expanded enough to stifle the entire house. So I left. Told Dad I was going over to Erin's, and shot out the front door.

It was easier to breathe outside.

Erin and I drove downtown to the mall. We looked around a bit and then headed for the food court. I found an empty table while Erin went to get us coffee. She slipped into a seat and slid a Styrofoam cup across the table to me.

"So, does this mean you're not mad at me after all?"

I shook the cobwebs out of my head. "What? Who said I was mad at you?"

Erin shrugged. "No one. But you haven't called in weeks and you're barely civil at school. Just like now. You're a space cadet. Earth to Kelly. You haven't said a coherent sentence all afternoon."

"Sorry."

Erin lifted both hands in the air. "See what I mean?" She put her hands down and stared at me. "If you're not mad at me, what's wrong? Does it have something to do with Sean?"

I shook my head. "No. Never mind. You don't want to know."

"Yes I do. But I guess you're entitled." She sounded hurt.

I sighed. "It's just Hannah. She's in trouble again, that's all." The thing was, I wasn't sure I wanted to tell Erin about what happened. Not that I didn't trust her to keep it to herself. But I was suddenly embarrassed.

"Okay," said Erin. "Let's talk about something else. Has Sean called you again?"

"Not since I told him I wasn't interested in the cross-country team."

Erin shook her head sadly. "You really blew that one."

I didn't think so. In fact, I was relieved. What if I'd gone out for the team or encouraged Sean, and he'd asked me out? I could see it all now. There he would be at the door; I'd have to introduce him to Hannah. "Oh, hey. Have you met my sister, you know, the juvenile delinquent?" What if Sean had been over at my place when the police came?

I immediately felt guilty for being so disloyal.

"It wasn't worth the effort," I told Erin.

"For crying out loud, Kelly," Erin said. "What effort? It's just a date."

Almost instantly I tuned her out. And Erin knew she'd gone too far.

"Hey, you. I'm sorry. C'mon. Tell me about Hannah. How am I supposed to be my understanding, sympathetic self if you don't tell me what's going on? What kind of trouble is she in?"

The sweet coffee left my mouth feeling sticky and stale. "Trouble with the police."

Erin's eyes opened wide. "Really? The police? What'd she do?"

I stared at the coffee in my cup and muttered, "They said she broke into a house. I don't know anything else."

"Is she doing all this because she doesn't like Caryn around?"

"Good question." The answer didn't seem as simple as that anymore. It was true that Hannah and Caryn argued a lot. But lately, Caryn left Dad to deal with her. When he wasn't around, she gave Hannah plenty of space. Instead of making things better, it just made them worse.

People shouldn't feel uncomfortable and on guard all the time in their own home.

The way Hannah refused to talk to Dad half the time was the worst. Dad and Hannah used to be so close. At one time I was even a little jealous of the way Dad seemed to treat her special, to take extra care with her.

I told myself it was because she was so young when Mom left and she needed more attention than I did. I was older and able to take care of myself better.

I remembered walking into our room one night, a few weeks after Mom moved out, to find Hannah busy pulling clothes out of her dresser.

"What are you doing?" I stood in the doorway in my pj's. "It's time to get ready for bed. Dad said he'd read us a story if we're ready when he comes up."

"I know," Hannah said. But she kept on doing what she was doing. She'd pick up a t-shirt, look at it, and then either toss it back in the drawer or fold it and put it on her bed. Curious, I walked over to take a closer look. There was an open suitcase on her bed, filled with clothes and stuffed animals. On top was a bag of chocolate chips and a box of Band Aids.

I looked at my sister in wonder. What was she up to now?!

"Are you running away?" I would never have thought of running away. But then Hannah was terribly brave. She was only six, and much braver than me.

"No," she scoffed. "That would be dumb. Who would take care of me?"

I bounced onto her bed and looked for clues in the

suitcase. She'd even packed her softest-ever. "Then what?"

"I'm just getting ready."

Sometimes Hannah could be so frustrating. "Ready for what?"

"I'm getting ready to go to the orphanage."

At first I thought she was joking. But no, she was gazing at me very seriously, her green eyes starting to get shiny and fill with tears until they looked like little puddles. She scrunched her lips together and tossed another t-shirt into the suitcase.

"Who said you were going to the orphanage?" I asked.

"Jenny. At school, Jenny said if your parents get divorced, the kids have to go to the orphanage. The orphanage is for kids without a mom and dad."

I have to admit, even though I was nine years old at the time, the way Hannah said it made me wonder if she might be right. I wanted to punch Jenny.

"Okay," I said. "Who's smarter, me or Jenny?"

"You." Her voice was confident.

"That's right. So you know what I say is right. And I say that Jenny is full of beans."

Hannah giggled, wiping her eyes. "She'd be awful stinky if she was full of beans."

"Well, she is. Just because Mom and Dad are getting divorced, it doesn't mean we don't have parents."

"How do you know?"

"I know." I tried to sound sure of myself. "There's lots of kids in my class that are divorced. Some of the them live with their moms, and some of them live with their dads."

"Where will we live?"

I sighed. "Dad said, remember? We're going to live with him, at least at first. Because Mom has to go places to take pictures. We'll see her in between times."

"Oh yeah. I remember."

"Good." I was glad that was settled. I got off her bed. "I'll help you unpack your suitcase."

"No," she said. "I'll just leave it. In case."

"In case what?"

"In case Dad has to go someplace, too."

"Dad is not going anywhere." I wasn't so sure of myself now. A sharp stab of fear stuck into my throat as I wondered what would happen if he did.

"I know. But what if? Then maybe we'd go to the orphanage."

"Fine. Suit yourself, then."

"I'll just keep my softest-ever with me." Hannah took the blanket out of her suitcase, closed it and pushed it under her bed.

"Okay," I said. "But you won't need the suitcase."

"Kelly?" Hannah crawled under her covers.

"Yeah."

"Mom could take pictures here."

"Yeah."

"Will you brush my hair for me until Daddy comes?"

"Yeah, okay." I tried to brush it the way I'd watched Mom do it, with long smooth strokes. But her thick brown hair was tangled and the brush kept getting stuck. It had obviously been a few days since her hair had been brushed properly. Dad must have forgot.

"Ow! That's not how you do it!" Hannah protested.

"I can't help it. Your hair is tangled."

"You're hurting me. Stop, stop, stop it! I want Mommy to do it!" She pushed me away and started to cry.

I was sitting there, wondering what to do, when Dad came in. "Hey, kidlets. What's this all about?"

"She won't let me brush her hair. It's all knotted up."

"I want Mom to do it!" Hannah said, screwing up her face.

Dad looked at her and scrunched his mouth a bit, almost like Hannah. He said, quietly, "Mom's not here, Hannah. Would you like me to brush your hair?"

Hannah stopped crying long enough to look up at Dad. "Can I phone her?"

"Me too?" I asked. "I want to talk to her, too."

Dad looked scared. Why is Dad scared? I wondered. Hannah started to cry again, and even I wanted to hide under the covers.

"Can we?" I asked. It was suddenly urgent that Hannah and I talk to Mom.

Dad sat down on Hannah's bed while I scooted over to make room for him. He took the brush from me and started to work on Hannah's hair. The brush handle disappeared in his big hands so it looked like his fingers were doing the work. "Tell you what. Tomorrow morning before school, we'll phone your mom. She'll be in Vancouver by then, and we can phone her at her hotel. Right now she's on an airplane. Would that be okay?"

I swallowed the panic that was growing inside me and nodded. Hannah calmed down a bit, too, but she wasn't very happy. Cell phones would have solved the problem, but back then cell phones weren't around.

"Are you ready for a story?" Dad asked. "You can choose, Hannah."

"The Saturday Night book," she said.

Dad smiled. I went and got the book of nursery rhymes and handed it to Dad. I was too old for nursery rhymes, but I was glad Hannah had asked for it. I still loved to hear Dad's strong voice recite the words.

Dad started to read; Hannah slipped onto his lap. He put his arm around her and rocked her while she looked at the pictures. By the time he got to Hannah's favorite poem, the one he always saved for last, she was nodding sleepily. "On Saturday night I lost my girl, and where do you think I found her?"

Hannah murmured, "Up in the moon, singing a tune."

"With all the stars around her," Dad finished.

"Again," said Hannah.

"On Saturday night I lost my girl, and where do you think I found her? Up in the moon, singing a tune, with all the stars around her."

Dad must have recited that rhyme ten times before Hannah fell asleep.

For a long time, the only way Hannah would go to sleep was if Dad rocked her in his arms and recited the Saturday Night poem. Even then she often crawled out of bed in the middle of the night and ran down the hall to Dad's room. Most of the time she'd come back, get into her bed and whisper to me, "He's asleep." Sometimes she didn't come back and Dad would find her curled up beside him in the morning.

The suitcase stayed under Hannah's bed. By the time Dad found it while he was spring cleaning, Hannah had outgrown most of the clothes she'd packed. Dad quietly put the clothes and the suitcase away.

Now, when Hannah and Dad talked at all, they just seemed to end up fighting.

"You really are a lost cause today." Erin's voice was only slightly impatient. She was playing with an empty coffee cup. "Getting you to talk is like pulling teeth."

I blinked, took a sip of my cold coffee. "I'm sorry." Erin was a good friend. And she wanted to help. "I was thinking about what you said. It's hard getting used to a stepmother, but I don't think that's what's bugging Hannah." I was thinking out loud. "It's almost like Dad is the one she's mad at, and she's using Caryn as an excuse to fight with him."

"Don't let it get to you," said Erin. "It's not your problem."

"I guess. There's nothing I can do about it anyway."

And there was no use worrying about things I couldn't control, I told myself.

12

Erin dropped me off just before dinner. "You can call anytime, you know. Or crash at my place if you really need to get away."

I nodded. "I know, Erin. Thanks."

Caryn was the only one home. I assumed that meant Dad and Hannah were at the police station. I headed upstairs, hoping not to be around when they got back. But then Caryn asked me to make a salad for dinner. Maybe she needed reinforcements.

I sliced veggies while Caryn put water on to boil for pasta, and made the sauce. The awkward silence was something I'd begun to expect, but that day Caryn wanted to talk.

"Kelly, do you know what's bothering Hannah?"

she asked.

"No. She's never done anything like this before. It's not like her."

Caryn laughed, a little bitterly. "You don't think so? I think it's exactly like her — not caring an iota about anyone else but herself."

It wasn't fair for her to talk about Hannah like that. Even if what she said sometimes seemed true. In a flash of annoyance, I said the first thing that popped into my head. "Hannah cares. She's trying not to, but she cares."

As soon as I heard my own words, I realized that they were at least partly true. It was as if Hannah was being as rotten as she could to prove that she didn't need us, to prove that we couldn't get to her. And just as suddenly, I recognized my own passive defence strategy flip into attack mode.

Maybe we weren't so different.

Caryn blushed. "You may be right. I'm sorry. I was out of line. I really don't know what Hannah was like before, and I know fourteen is a difficult age. I just never expected anything like this."

I nodded and kept slicing. She was doing it again. Nudging into my space, trying to get me to sympathize.

I was setting the table when the car pulled into the driveway. Caryn took a deep breath and smiled weakly at me. We waited, awkward. I didn't know how to act, what to say. But then Hannah and Dad were too busy yelling at each other to notice.

Dad followed Hannah into the house. "You got off goddamned lucky, kid! What did you expect?"

"I don't expect anything, okay? I don't need your help, I don't want your help!"

"I didn't see anyone else waiting anxiously to save you from yourself. No one likes being stepped on, Hannah."

"You don't know anything!" Hannah screamed at him.

"Maybe I don't!" Dad yelled right back. "But I know you have no respect, no appreciation for people who are trying to help you. Maybe I should've let you spend the night in jail!"

"That would've been better than being here!" Hannah noticed Caryn and me standing together by the table, gave us a look of complete contempt, then ran up the stairs and slammed her bedroom door.

Dad was trembling, drawing hard, raspy breaths. He slumped down in a chair. "Well, that went well."

"Is she okay?" Caryn asked.

"Who knows? I think she's mostly angry that she got caught." Then he sighed. "But maybe I'm wrong, maybe she's just scared. I lost it. Let's leave her alone for a while."

Scared? It never occurred to me that Hannah might be scared of something.

"What happened?" I asked.

Dad waved his hand with this feeble, defeated kind of gesture. "Not now, Kelly, okay?" He looked so tired, so let down. I wanted to go over and put my arms around him and tell him that I loved him. I wanted to, but I couldn't. He was there; I was here. I didn't know how to cross the gap.

Caryn did, though. She stood behind his chair and

put her arms around his neck. Dad reached up and held her hand. And I felt myself moving even further away from them, fading into the background of what they were sharing. I started to leave; Dad's voice called me back.

"Are you still running, Kelly?"

I shrugged. "Some. Not too much."

"Let's go for a run tomorrow morning, then. I miss running with you."

And I missed running with him. "Sure." I smiled weakly. "Okay."

After dinner, while Dad and Caryn did the dishes, I went out on the roof to watch the nighthawks. One was flying over our back yard, almost, just behind the alley. It looked a bit spastic — its wings beating to no regular rhythm — as though it took a desperate struggle just to lift itself into the air. I cringed as the bird plunged toward the ground. One of these times it was going to go too far, wait an instant too long, be hurtling too fast to pull out. Between the swooping bird and the ground was nothing but the turn of a few feathers.

I'd made one hurried check in the computer catalog at our school library, looking for a book about nighthawks, but nothing had turned up. With the wedding and then exams, I'd been too busy to do a more thorough search. I didn't have my marks yet, but I was pretty sure my average would be in the high 80s. I might even nudge past the 90 percent mark.

Hannah, on the other hand, had brought her report card home on the last day of school earlier that week.

She passed, barely, which was pretty good considering that she only went to about half the classes.

I didn't know anymore whether I felt mad at her, or sorry for her. I suppose both feelings were mixed up together. Sympathy pains drew me back into the house and up to her bedroom door. I didn't relish the thought of her throwing a fit at me, but — she was my sister. I tapped gently on her door. "Hannah. It's me. Can I come in?"

When there was no answer, I opened the door a few inches. She was lying on the floor beside her bed, stuffing something up under the box spring. I caught a glimpse of what looked like a box.

Hannah saw me and scrambled to her feet. "Get lost," she said fiercely. "Don't you ever touch my stuff." She stared at me with this hard look in her eyes, but her face was blotchy red from crying. Maybe Dad was right; maybe she was scared.

My heart was thumping like crazy as I stepped into her room, closed the door and stood there with my back against it, wondering what I was doing, wondering what to say. Finally, I just opened my mouth and trusted the words to come out right. "I don't know what's going on, but I'm sorry."

She made a funny sound from deep inside, something between a gasp and a sob, and sank down on her bed. I went and sat beside her.

"I hate my life," she said.

I didn't know how to answer that. I didn't really believe her.

"It was just a dare," she continued. "We were sitting

around and someone said he knew this kid who was playing in a ball tournament out of town this weekend and his parents had gone with him, so no one was home. And someone else said the house would be locked and, anyway, no one had the guts to break in. And I said, 'I did.'"

"You said what? Why did you say that?"

"I don't know. I just said it. Everyone looked at me and said, 'Yeah, sure,' and then somebody said they knew people who would pay us for stuff and dared me to do it. So I did."

"Who dared you?"

She stiffened. "Never mind."

"Was it Natalie?"

"Forget it. I wouldn't tell the cops and I'm sure not going to tell you."

"Okay, okay. So what happens now?"

"I don't know. Ian was some kind of mad. He hates me. What else is new."

That was too ridiculous to be worth a response. "I mean, what happens with the police? Do you have to go to court?"

"No. They said something about because it was my first offence, I wouldn't have to."

"Well, that's good, isn't it?"

She didn't answer.

"Well, isn't it?"

"I don't care. I'll have to do community service or something. I have to go see a probation officer next week."

I shook my head. "Hannah, come on. Dad's right.

You got off easy."

She gave me a disgusted look. "I wasn't the only one there, you know. I was just the only one who got caught. Lots of kids are doing far worse stuff."

"You could have told the police about the others."

"Yeah, right. I'm not squealing on my friends. Not everyone enjoys being a hermit like you."

"I'm not a hermit."

"Bull, Kelly. You're seventeen and you spend most of your weekends at home reading or stuck in your darkroom. My friends think you're weird." She stood up and wiped her hands across her face. "Not my idea of a life."

"You just said you hated your life." If she was going to attack, I could defend myself.

"I wouldn't if people would just leave me alone. If Ian and Caryn would just quit picking on me and trying to run my life. They don't even like my friends. At least I have friends. At least they want me around."

Any sympathy I had was giving way to anger. Some friends, I thought. How could Hannah be so blind and so stubborn? "So how come you got caught and no one else did?"

Hannah looked a little puzzled. "I don't know. Some kid from school saw me and recognized me, but I don't know him." She flopped back down on her bed and stared up at the ceiling. "It's not fair. Ian and Caryn will probably ground me forever. Ian wouldn't even talk to me on the way home from the police station; when he did, he started yelling. He could hardly wait for me to get out of his sight. He'd send me to live with

Mom if he could. I wish he would. At least then there wouldn't always be someone telling me what to do."

"Get real," I said. "Like that's going to happen. And how do you expect Dad to react? He's home for all of one week, and you pull something like this. Great way to start summer vacation."

"I should've known you'd take their side." But her voice didn't have any mad left in it. It was tired and empty. "Why don't you just leave me alone?"

This was turning out just like I expected. I didn't need it. I got up to leave.

"Kelly," Hannah whispered.

"Yeah?"

"I wish Mom was here." She was crying now, and trying not to.

My own anger drained away. I was suddenly empty and exhausted, too. "She'd be just as mad."

"I guess. But it wouldn't seem so bad, if everything was the way it used to be, if people and things didn't change all the time. I wish I was still little and didn't know — didn't know anything. It's easier if you don't know things."

"Yeah." Instead of leaving, I picked up Hannah's hairbrush from the dresser. "You're a mess. Sit up and I'll brush your hair for you."

She sat up absently. "Did you ever think that Dad got stuck with us when they divorced? That he didn't really want us but he had no choice?"

I pulled the brush through her hair in long, slow strokes and took my time answering, choosing my words carefully because it was so easy to say the wrong thing to Hannah these days. "I think it was hard for Mom to give custody of us to Dad. I think she did it because she thought he'd be able to take better care of us, not because she didn't want us herself. And I think Dad agreed with her. It was about the only thing they did agree on."

"But still, Dad didn't really have a choice, did he?"

Maybe she was right in a way, but I seemed to remember Dad being pretty adamant about getting custody. He did want us. Hannah might not be able to remember all those words that came up the stairs in the dark, but I did. "He had a choice. People always have a choice. He could have sent us to live with Granny and Gramps. I remember that's what they wanted, but he said 'no.'"

"Maybe, but now he's chosen Caryn." Her voice was tired and soft. She didn't expect an answer, and I didn't have one.

"The color of the wind," I murmured.

"Hmmm?"

"Your hair," I said. "Remember the game we used to play? It's the color of the wind."

Hannah just sighed and was quiet. After a while she said, her voice hard again, "So is dirt."

I kept on brushing, staring at nothing until the room went hazy and out of focus. Somewhere, far away, it seemed to me that I saw Hannah tumbling down from the moon, all the stars trembling around her.

wrong thing to him if these days, "I think it was hard for him to get rid of his fear.

Why I Don't Want to be a Criminal
by Hannah Farrell

There are plenty of reasons I don't want to be a criminal. Lousy food is one. Not that I know for a fact that prison food is lousy, but when meals are made for lots of people, the food is usually overcooked. Like in the school cafeteria. With my luck they probably serve lots of cream corn in jail. I hate cream corn. I hate mushy vegetables of any kind. And cardboard hamburgers. And plastic cheese.

Then there are the public showers. I'm not ever taking a shower with a whole pile of other people. And no one is going to strip search this body! Unless you're a dentist putting in a filling, my body cavities are off limits.

I don't think they have toilets in your cell where everyone can see you like they sometimes show on TV. I think there are real bathrooms and the cells are little rooms. But they lock you up at night and I heard you have to go to school or work during the day, too. Going to jail would be like being grounded. Only you wouldn't have the comforts of your own room or be able to watch TV when you want. When my friends or family came to visit, I wouldn't be able to go out to a movie with them or spend the day on the beach or anything. Unless I got a weekend pass.

Even after I got out of jail, I might not be able to leave the country so I'd never get to go to Hawaii or Mexico or Europe or Australia. Or anywhere.

Not all criminals hurt people. When you steal things, people usually have insurance that pays to replace the things you stole. So no one gets hurt except the insurance companies and that's what they are there for. I know stealing is still wrong and everything, but I think crimes that hurt people are more wrong than crimes that don't hurt anyone. Lying isn't even a crime and it can hurt people more than stealing.

I don't want to be a criminal because people think you're a bad person even if you're not and treat you different. They think they know you but they don't. They don't like you. They sure don't trust you. I don't know for sure, why it is important for people to like you, but it is.

13

The police didn't charge Hannah, but only because she agreed to complete an alternative measures program. She had been right about having to do community service. Forty hours worth, plus write an essay on why she didn't want to be a criminal.

"This is so dumb," she said, staring at the computer's screen saver as it made psychedelic whirls across the screen. But it was either write the essay or go to court.

Marge was Hannah's supervisor at the nursing home where she was assigned her community service. I met her when I gave Hannah a ride one day, about a week after she started. Dad was back at work and

Caryn was busy making appetizers for a reception she was catering that afternoon. Somehow life kept going as usual.

I couldn't detect any activity when I pulled up in front of the manicured lawns of the nursing home. Then I saw someone nodding in a chair under the shaded front entrance.

"What time should I pick you up?" I asked Hannah.

"I'll call," she said, slamming the car door.

I watched her trot up the stairs, pausing in front of the sleeping old man to wave her hands in front of his face. He didn't move. She looked at me, shrugged and went inside.

When I went to pick her up later she wasn't waiting out front, so I parked the car and went inside. As soon as I walked in the door, the lazy, warm smell of summer gave way to a stale, antiseptic odor. The place smelled dormant, like it was waiting for something to nudge it awake.

I asked for Hannah and a nurse at the reception area pointed me in the direction of the recreation room. I stood in the doorway and looked around. There were two sofas and a couple of chairs in front of a TV in one corner. In the middle of the room was a shuffleboard table. Old people, mostly women, were sitting at some tables on the other side of the room, working on crafts of one kind or another. In the far corner was a piano, the keyboard cover firmly closed.

A row of game tables stood along the opposite wall, a deck of cards on one table, checkerboards and crokinole boards on others. Hannah was sitting at one of the tables, playing checkers with a tall, thin old man. He was absently scratching the inside of his ear and running his fingers through unruly tufts of white hair.

"She'll be finished in a few minutes," a voice said at my elbow. I turned to find a woman standing beside me. "Mr. Fletcher over there insisted on another game, and Hannah was nice enough to oblige him. I'm Marge Neufeld."

"Hi," I said. "I'm Kelly." I hesitated and added, "Hannah's sister." Marge's short-cropped dark hair framed a round face with loads of crinkles around her eyes and mouth; you could see she laughed a lot. I liked her immediately.

"Hannah said you'd be coming." Marge nodded toward the checkers table. "Your sister is a godsend. She has real talent. It's the first time Mr. Fletcher has sat still for more than five minutes since his son canceled their holiday plans."

I didn't know what she was talking about at first. "I didn't know she even played checkers," I said.

Marge laughed. "No, not checkers. Watch. Make yourself at home." She turned to leave, putting her hand on my arm as she did. "I have to run. Hope to see you again." I got the feeling she meant it.

Hannah nodded at me as I walked over and sat down near the game tables to watch her and this Fletcher guy play checkers.

The old man leaned over the table, glanced sideways and whispered to Hannah, "Hey, Chickie. You a bettin' girl?"

Hannah mimicked him, leaning across the table

so that their two heads almost touched. "First of all, Fletch, for the umpteenth time, my name is Hannah, not Chickie. Second, prepare to get your butt kicked, old man."

"Hurt you more'n me," he chuckled. "My butt's kinda bony."

Hannah leaned over and looked at his butt. "Not so bad," she said, "for an old guy."

Fletch shook his head sorrowfully, but I could see the gleam in his eye. "No respect, Chickie," he said. "You got no respect. But I'll teach you some."

"I can hardly wait," Hannah said. "Set 'em up."

"Hey, hey, hey. Slow down, Chickie. Let's see some cash. Just because I'm an old fart stuck in this god-forsaken, wrinkle-infested, incontinent, Pine Sol purgatory, doesn't mean I'm gonna let some sweet young thing pull one over on me."

I suppressed a snicker, not so much at his language as at the idea of Hannah as a sweet young thing. That was definitely one view I'd never had of her before.

Hannah didn't even miss a beat. She reached into her pocket and pulled out a handful of loonies and a crumpled two-dollar bill.

Fletcher raised his eyebrows. "That's pretty near a collector's item, Chickie. Sure you want to lose it?"

"I have no intention of losing it, but thanks for worrying. I've got six dollars. Is that enough to get into this game or not?"

"That'll be jus' fine, Chickie. Jus' fine." He went to make the opening move.

"Hey, hey, hey," Hannah said. "Where's your cash,

Fletch?"

The old guy spluttered. "Why, you nervy little bugger. I should have let the blue-hairs dearie you to death. I'm good for it."

Hannah just tapped the table with her finger. "Right here, Fletch. Cold, hard cash."

Fletch smiled as he dug some money out of his pocket and pushed it under Hannah's nose. He put it back in his pocket. "Satisfied, Chickie?"

Hannah nodded and they settled down to play. After the first few moves, Fletch started to take his time.

"Hokay, Fletch, it's your turn," Hannah coaxed him.

"Hey, hey, hey. Don't get your rope tied in a knot, Chickie," he muttered.

Hannah rolled her eyes and sat back. When he finally did go to pick up one of his checkers, she groaned. "Fletch, my *Nana* would whop your butt if you played like that with her."

The guy snorted. He picked up his checker and jumped one of Hannah's. She immediately double-jumped him back. "I told you," she said.

"Dirty dihedralized dora," he fumed.

"Don't know her," Hannah came back immediately.

Fletch suddenly cackled in delight and jumped one of Hannah's checkers to get a king. "Your mother!" he gloated.

"Don't know her, either," Hannah said, more quietly this time.

The old guy gave her the evil eye. "Your move, Chickie."

Hannah took her turn and leaned back again. "This

is the nineties, fella. Don't you know you're not allowed to call a woman 'Chickie'?"

"I'm *in* my nineties. Don't you know I'm not responsible? Besides, what are you going to do about it, Chickie?" He chuckled and nudged one of his checkers forward.

"Wipe you off the board," Hannah said, and proceeded to do just that. "There, old man. Last game is mine. Pay up."

"Bomakle!" Fletch muttered, but he fumbled for his cash and slapped it into her hand. She got up.

"Gotta go. See ya later, dude. Next time, don't make me mad."

"Hey, Chickie," Fletch called after her.

She turned. "Yeah?"

"Next time, bring that Nana of yours along. So long as she don't have blue hair, that is."

"In your dreams, Fletch." She walked away, grinning.

Hannah finished her forty hours in two weeks, spending a few hours almost every day at the nursing home. She even went back for a couple of days after she'd finished, so that she could help with a birthday party they were giving Mr. Fletcher.

Between basketball camp and community service hours, Hannah was busy most of July. I began to think she was getting mellow in the warmth of summer. She at least figured out that she had to be home by curfew if she wanted to go out again the next night. Maybe it was just that there was less pressure with no school, or that Dad wasn't home to fight with. Caryn was giving Hannah a lot of space.

Even during that lull in the storm, I guess I suspected Hannah had only gotten better at deceiving people, and that maybe we were deceiving ourselves. I know that I was, and I think Dad and Caryn, and Mom probably were, too. I was just happy Hannah didn't do anything to jeopardize the holiday we had planned with Mom and Peter.

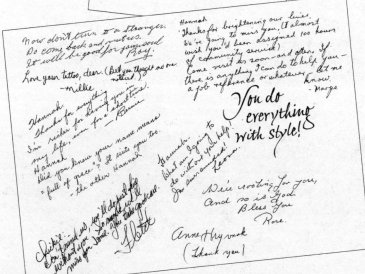

Now don't turn to a stranger.
Do come back and see us.
So will be good for your soul.
Roy.

Love your tattoo, deer. (Bet you thought no one
~ Millie   ~ Millred.)

Hannah,
Thanks for everything.
I'm richer for having you in
my life, even for a short time. - Renie

Hannah,
Did you know your name means
"full of grace"? It suits you too.
~ the other Hannah

Jackie:
Don't remind us, we'll do just fine
without you. So maybe we'll
miss you some. Take good care.
~ Nlotti

Hannah,
Thanks for brightening our lives.
We're going to miss you. (I almost
wish you'd been assigned 100 hours
of community service.)
Come visit us soon—and often. If
there is anything I can do to help you—
a job reference or whatever. Let me
know.
~ Marge

You do
everything
with style!

Hannah,
What am I going to
do without your help!
Jos awwanged it.
Leona.

We're rooting for you,
And so is God.
Bless You.
Rose.

Anne Hryvnak
(Thank you)

121

skinDeep
TAttOO

NUMBER _____ DATE *Nov 6* _____ 19 *98*		
RECEIVED FROM *Taylar Dormaar*		
THE SUM OF *Seventy five* _____ /100 DOLLARS		
G.S.T. _____ *5.25*		
FOR *Small Group B*		

BY CASH ☑	PER	$
BY CHEQUE ☐		80 25

N°· 1146509   CUSTOMER'S COPY – RECEIPT

14

Mom was the one who discovered Hannah's tattoo, during our camping trip to Montana.

It was the beginning of August, and hot. I was glad to be in the mountains for a while, away from the dry, blistering heat scorching the prairie to a crackling pale version of itself. Even in the mountains, it was so hot that the icy streams pouring down from the glaciers looked awfully tempting, especially after hiking all day. On the way back to camp in the late afternoon, toward the end of our holiday, Mom stopped the car beside a spot where the stream cascaded around and over a rock ledge into a deep, clear green pool.

She grinned at Hannah and me. "Dare you."

"You're on!" Hannah laughed, almost her old self

for a moment. "If we get wet, you have to, too."

We wore bathing suits under our clothes on holidays, and it took us about five seconds to slip off our hiking shorts and t-shirts.

"Not me!" Mom said. "Peter can be my proxy."

Peter groaned, but Hannah and I practically pulled him out of the car and down the path to the rock slabs above the pool. Mom followed with towels.

Nothing much had changed during the holiday as far as Hannah was concerned. She kept quiet except for brief moments like this when she forgot to stay in the role of angry, persecuted teenager. She spent most of her time watching Mom, which made for a weird tension between the two of them, not at all like our usual visits.

But today the hot sun and the shimmering pool were enough to loosen anyone's resolve, including Hannah's. The jumble of rock slabs beside the stream was a warm, lazy place. The water rushing by was cool green. I sat on the edge of a rock, feeling its heat against my legs, and dangled my feet in the icy water. In a couple of seconds I pulled my feet out, tingling with cold.

"No turning back!" Hannah shouted. She stood poised on the edge of a rock ledge above the pool — a memory surfaced briefly of her poised on the edge of the roof — then flashed a crooked grin, and jumped. She surfaced in a couple of seconds and waved at me. "C'mon. It's not that bad."

I was hot and sticky with sweat from hiking. I slid into the pool and waded out to my waist, feeling the current tug at my legs. Closing my eyes, I lifted my legs, ducked under the surface and came up just as quickly, gasping for breath. The icy water seemed to flow right through me and seize hold of my heart. In two quick strokes I was back at the shore, pulling my numb body onto the sun-warmed rocks.

Hannah followed me out of the water, laughing. "Your turn, Peter." He looked a little dubious. "C'mon. It's not that cold, see?" She jumped in again and hoisted herself out on the rocks, dripping.

I was shivering so hard I couldn't talk. Hannah didn't even have goosebumps. By now there was a small crowd gathered at the roadside pullout, watching us. Other people were making their way down with towels. Hannah scrambled to her rocky perch and jumped again.

It was enough to convince Peter. He waited for Hannah to return and the two of them jumped together. By now I was able to hold a camera in my hands and I snapped a photo of them in midair.

Peter came up with his eyes wide and his face white. "Oh, man," he gasped, swimming for shore.

Hannah laughed. "You're showing your age, Peter."

He joined me on the warm rocks and sat wrapped in a towel while Hannah took one more jump. I snapped a series of photos of her on the rock ledge, splashing into the pool and pulling herself out on the rocks. That's when we saw the tattoo.

"What is that?" Mom sounded incredulous. She stared as Hannah scrambled out of the water.

Hannah immediately grabbed her towel and

wrapped it around her middle. "Nothing. Probably scraped myself on a rock."

"Hannah Jayne Farrell."

"Okay, okay. Don't make a fuss, Mom. It's a tattoo. Here, see?"

Mom, Peter and I stared at the small patch of color etched into Hannah's hip, half covered by her swim suit bottom.

I was shivering again. "A real tattoo?" I breathed through chattering teeth.

"Of course a real tattoo. I think I'm a little old for stick-ons."

"Did it hurt?" This was totally fascinating. My sister had a tattoo. A real tattoo. There were quite a few kids at school getting them, but most of them had to use fake I.D. because you were supposed to be eighteen.

Hannah grimaced. "Oh, yeah."

Mom still hadn't said a word. She looked at the tattoo, she looked at Hannah, she looked back at the tattoo. She turned and walked away.

"Uh-oh," Hannah said.

"Oh, yeah," I agreed.

Hannah turned to Peter. "Tell her it's not a big deal, okay, Peter? See, it healed nicely, no infection. I took good care of it."

"Not me, Hannah. I'm not getting in the middle of this one. You talk to her." He glanced after Mom's retreating back. "But I'd recommend you wait just a bit."

Back in the car, I got Hannah to give me a closer look at her tattoo. "Road Runner? You got the Road Runner tattooed on your stomach?" The Road Runner was going flat out, legs churning around Hannah's hip bone.

"Yeah," said Hannah. "I like him. Nothing slows him down."

Mom stiffened in the front seat.

"Tattoos cost money," I whispered. "Where did you get the money?"

"I had it saved, from birthdays and stuff."

I knew she was lying.

There wasn't much Mom could do besides give Hannah a stinging lecture when we got back to camp. It went sort of like, "I've seen some stupid stunts in my life, but this one takes the cake. Do you realize this is permanent, as in forever? You will go through your entire life with a bird on your belly. What were you thinking?"

Followed by more of the same.

"Does your father know about this?" she asked.

"No." Hannah listened meekly through another tirade until Mom ran out of breath. Then she asked quietly, "Would you like it better if it said 'Mother'?"

Peter almost fell in the fire and I nearly choked on my hot dog, we laughed so hard. Hannah gave Mom an uncertain grin and soon even Mom couldn't keep a completely straight face. She looked at Hannah a little strange, as if she couldn't figure out if she was joking or not, and then laughed awkwardly.

"You will tell your father when you get home," she ordered. "Promise me. You can't keep something like this from him. You should go to a doctor and make sure there's no infection."

Hannah nodded. "Sure, Mom. I promise. You can trust me." There wasn't an ounce of humor left in her voice. "We wouldn't want to have any secrets in this family, would we, Mom?" Hannah almost sounded like Dad when he was close to losing it. Her eyes shone queerly in the light of the campfire. She jumped up suddenly. "I'm going to get some firewood for the morning." She walked off, leaving dead silence behind her.

"What was that all about?" Mom turned to me.

I didn't have a clue. I shook my head. "She's decided it's her against the world. She's always flipping out on everyone."

"There has to be a reason." Mom was peering into the dark where Hannah had disappeared.

I shrugged. "Don't ask me. Ask her." I was not going to let Hannah's turmoil intrude into my holiday. I stuck a marshmallow on a stick and held it near the fire where it would turn a smooth golden brown on the outside, and just barely go soft on the inside. Hannah always stuck her marshmallow right into the flames until it caught fire. She let it burn into charcoal on the outside before blowing it out and peeling off the burnt layer with her fingers.

But Hannah wasn't into roasting marshmallows that night. When she got back, she dumped the firewood under the picnic table, mumbled something about being tired and disappeared again into our tent. She was asleep, or pretending to be asleep, by the time I joined her.

She avoided being alone with Mom the last two days of our holiday, just like she avoided Dad at home.

Finally Mom shook her head and said it must be hormones and that we'd have to wait until Hannah was ready to tell us what was bugging her. Then she left for Vancouver Island, where she was shooting photos for an article on the fishing industry.

We didn't have long to wait.

Dad's welding rig was in the driveway when we got home. While we were away, it turned out, the police had come by again. Looking for Hannah.

**CAUTION AND WAIVER PURSUANT TO THE YOUNG OFFENDERS ACT
PRIOR TO TAKING OF A STATEMENT**

NAME OF YOUNG PERSON   *HANNAH FARRELL*   DOB: 25/11/83

A. BEFORE YOU SAY OR WRITE ANYTHING, I MUST TELL YOU THAT:
1. You do not have to say or write anything.
2. Anything you say or write may be used as evidence against you.
3. You have the right to speak to a lawyer, a parent, an adult relative OR any adult person you choose.
4. If you want to say or write anything, the person you choose must be present unless you do not want that person there.

I HAVE BEEN TOLD ABOUT MY RIGHTS AND I UNDERSTAND THEM.

Hannah Farrell
Young Person's Signature

**B. DO YOU WANT TO TALK TO A LAWYER, A PARENT, AN ADULT RELATIVE OR ANY
OTHER ADULT BEFORE YOU SAY OR WRITE ANYTHING?**

☑ YES   If yes, a reasonable opportunity to talk to an adult of the young person's choice must be given to the young person.

☐ No   **Waiver:** I have been told that before I write or say anything, I must be given a reasonable opportunity to speak to a lawyer and to a parent or adult of my choice. I do not wish to speak to any of these persons before I say or write anything.

Hannah Farrell
Young Person's Signature

**C. DO YOU WANT TO HAVE THAT PERSON PRESENT WHILE YOU SAY OR WRITE
ANYTHING?**

☐ YES   If yes, a reasonable opportunity to say or write anything in the presence of that person must be provided.

☑ No   **Waiver:** I have talked to *Ian Farrell*, *Father* (relationship) and I have been told and I understand that I must be given a reasonable opportunity to have that person present while I say or write anything. I do not want that person present while I say or write anything.

Hannah Farrell
Young Person's Signature

Place: *Black Diamond P.S.*   *Cst. J Warren*
Date: *Aug 9/98*   Time: *19:20*   Police Officer's Signature

Black Diamond Police Service
STATEMENT CONTINUATION

PAGE _1_ OF _2_

    I was out with my friends that Saturday. I guess it was July 18. We were at the Park, just hanging out. Playing catch, roasting hot dogs, listening to music, that kind of stuff. No one was drinking that I know of, except maybe we had one beer each. Then we started playing this game, sort of like spin the bottle. When the bottle pointed at you, other people would dare you to do something. The dare had to be something serious, you know, risky. One person had to climb the fence into the pool and swim two lengths. Every dare had to be more risky than the last. By the time it was my turn, I had to sneak into one of the houses along the park, and bring something out to prove I had really done it. So I walked along the back alley and snuck into the back yard of this house. No one was home and a window was open. I moved a patio table under the window, climbed on the chair and pushed the screen out. I didn't mean to tear the screen. That was an accident.

SIGNED: _Cst. J. Warren_   SIGNED: _Tamara Farrell_
    INTERVIEWING OFFICER   **PERSON GIVING STATEMENT**

Black Diamond Police Service
STATEMENT CONTINUATION
PAGE 2 OF 2

    I was in a hurry and I opened the cupboard and cabinet
doors until I found where they kept their liquor and I took
a couple of bottles. They had lots so I didn't think they
would miss it, and I figured I might as well take something
we could use. I went out the front door but I dropped one of
the bottles and it smashed on the sidewalk and so I ran.

    That's it. There isn't anything more to tell. There was
no one else with me when I snuck into the house. The others
were waiting across the street in the park, but I don't
remember who was there that night. Maybe I had more to drink
than I thought. It was just a game and I was the loser. I
didn't think it would hurt anyone, but I know it was wrong.

    I don't know why the stereo and VCR were disconnected.
The people who lived there must have done that. Maybe they
planned to move stuff around.

SIGNED: _Cst. J. Warren_
INTERVIEWING OFFICER

SIGNED: _Hannah Farrell_
PERSON GIVING STATEMENT

15

Caryn had called Dad after the visit from the police. He'd got in his truck, drove home and was waiting for us when we got back from our camping trip. Hannah never even got a chance to unpack. Dad let her shower and change and then took her to the police station. The police questioned her and took her statement.

Then they charged her with breaking-and-entering.

Dad tossed his keys on the table when they got home and muttered, "Court on Wednesday. I'll get her a lawyer tomorrow."

Hannah slunk upstairs to her room without a word. Dad got a beer from the fridge and went outside to sit in the back yard. Caryn went with him.

The house was silent. Our holiday was over, just

like that.

Try as I might to stay oblivious to everything, it was pretty much impossible to ignore the fact that Hannah was out of control — on a downhill run headed nowhere. And the rest of us were along for the ride.

I felt sick, sitting out on the roof, my knees hugged tight against me. At least out here the silence didn't sound so much like despair. I stayed on the roof for a long time, searching for the nighthawks and listening for the familiar sound of their dives.

But even the nighthawks were silent.

At first I thought they'd moved on. Eventually, I spotted them flying above the pond at the far end of the field, darting back and forth, this way and that. I waited for them to climb into the sky and dive for me again, but they stayed close to the ground.

Twilight crept forward, crickets began to sing; after a while, quiet voices floated up from the back yard, lifted by the warm air of day rising off the ground.

"Are you going to tell me what happened?" Caryn asked.

"She told them it was a game, and that she was alone, but the police don't believe her," Dad said. "They're pretty sure that when Hannah dropped the bottles, the others got spooked and took off before they had a chance to take the stereo equipment."

"Maybe she's scared of them."

"Maybe." Dad's voice was bitter. "Maybe she's just protecting her friends."

"So what will happen to her?"

"Not much, probably. She's not eligible for the

alternative measures program a second time, so she's going to court. But it's a first offence."

"The first time she's been caught, you mean."

"Whatever. It was a mistake for me to take this job. I'm gone too much." Dad's voice broke and his words tumbled headlong over each other. "Everything I do when it comes to Hannah is wrong. I can't get through to her. The two of you are barely speaking. Kelly is distancing herself from all of us. Maybe we got married too soon. Maybe we should have given the girls more time to get used to the idea. Maybe the wedding on top of everything else was all too much for Hannah."

I hardly believed the person saying those things was my father. Dad never wasted energy on second-guessing himself. It was part of what made him so dependable.

I tried to concentrate on watching the sky behind the nighthawks change color as the sun went down — on finding and holding on to the separate parts of the sunset. White, feather-wisps of clouds glowed pastel pink and yellow, while the soft blue of the sky deepened. Then the clouds darkened to rose and the sky became pale, washed out, as if the clouds had sucked the color right out of it. Finally, the colors faded altogether. The clouds were grey spectres stretched across a blank sky. The birds, further out now, became dusty specks, tossed about aimlessly by the wind.

All of it, I thought, the color of wind. Even the voices; pale and thin, with a ragged edge.

"Are you saying that we're a mistake, too?"

"No, I didn't mean —"

Caryn cut Dad off. "She's your kid, not mine. You can't expect me to put up with all this."

"That's right, she's mine." Dad's voice was flat, matter of fact. "And so is Kelly. I'm not about to give up on either of them."

The silence was longer this time.

"I'm sorry. I didn't mean that," Caryn said. "Look, if I had any answers, I'd give them to you. But I don't know what to think anymore. I only know I can't take it much longer."

"I have to leave again," said Dad, gently. "If I don't go back I can forget about ever getting another pipeline job." Now he was apologizing to her.

"When?"

"I can stay for court on Wednesday morning, but then I have to get back. I've pushed the limits of my friendship with Jack. If he wasn't foreman, I'd have been kicked off the job a long time ago."

I wondered how long Dad would be gone this time. As if he was reading my mind, he said, "I'll be home by Thanksgiving. I've already got some leads on a couple of jobs coming up closer to home. We just have to make it through this."

"I'm not sure I can deal with Hannah for that long on my own."

"A trip to court has got to wake her up. Maybe it will turn out to be a good thing, if it gets her turned around."

A nighthawk fluttered over the light in the alley. The chorus of crickets was warming up.

"I'm scared, Ian. I'm scared for Hannah." Caryn sounded close to tears. "But I'm even more scared for us."

Dad laughed an odd, choking kind of laugh. "Look at us. What a pair."

Caryn sniffed and tried to laugh with him. "Maybe we need to get some help."

"Maybe you're right."

I didn't want to listen to the hurt in Dad's voice, to hear him admit he couldn't cope. My sanctuary wasn't safe tonight. I went back inside and down into my darkroom to develop the film I shot on our holiday. By the time the four rolls of negatives were hanging up to dry an hour later, everyone else was in bed.

I snuck up to my room, grateful for the darkness that closed around me.

16

The next morning I left the house early, not waiting for Dad, not knowing how to be close to him right now, and not wanting to be anywhere near Hannah or Caryn.

I went for a long run — a couple of times through the neighborhood, then down past the firehall and out onto the highway. With Dad gone all summer, I hadn't done much running. I was out of shape and became winded quickly. Each breath began to sear my throat and lungs, but I kept going. The physical pain was a relief.

I had slowed to an easy jog down the last block before home when, almost as if on cue, Sean appeared.

"Hey, Kelly," he said, falling in smoothly beside me and slowing his pace to match mine. "You pulled a disappearing act this summer. Have you been away a lot?"

I glanced sideways at him. "What do you do? Wait for me every morning?"

He grinned. "I would, if I thought you'd run with me. But you probably couldn't keep up."

He wasn't going to find it that easy to goad me into running with him. "Don't you ever give up?"

He thought about it. "Let's say I recover from rejection easily. But if I don't make some progress I'll eventually get discouraged. Then you'll be sorry."

"I'll be the judge of that." I bit my lip as I said it, but it was too late.

Sean's long hair was pulled back in a ponytail that swung around as he shook his head. "Man, you are hard to get through to. I just thought we had enough in common to be friends. That it would be nice to have someone to run with."

I was glad my already flushed face hid my reaction. I stammered out something about catching me on a bad day and not meaning to be rude. "I'm sure you're really a nice guy and everything . . ."

"Yeah," he said. "I am."

"Maybe some other time, okay?"

"Okay. I'll call that progress." He reached over and tucked a loose sweaty strand of hair behind my ear. Then he smiled lopsidedly; a nice, friendly smile. "Hope you don't mind. I just had to do that."

When I got back, I stood under the shower until the hot water ran out, totally confused. Dad was just in from his own run when I came downstairs again. "Missed you this morning," he said, a question in his eyes.

"I couldn't sleep," I mumbled. "Went out early." Then, not wanting to hurt him more, I added, "How about tomorrow?"

I grabbed some breakfast and watched Dad and Caryn move zombie-like through the morning. Hannah still hadn't made an appearance. Today, I decided, would be a good time to look up some information about nighthawks. I wanted to find out why they'd stopped diving, but mostly it was a good excuse to get away from the hollow tomb that the house had become.

It was already hot out. I took my time, riding my bike leisurely to the public library, dawdling as much as possible along the way.

There wasn't any listing for nighthawks in the library's computer catalog. I checked subject and title headings, but the only thing that came up was some novel about a sax player. Eventually, feeling frustrated and restless and heavy-headed, and wanting to be back in the open air again, I checked out a couple of books about hawks and a general field guide to birds to browse through at home.

There was no relief outside. The day had grown stifling; even the breeze burned my face as I cycled. I detoured to Erin's to let her know I was back from holidays, and stayed for something cold to drink. We lounged in the shade of her back yard while I brought her up to date. Erin was easy to talk to; she didn't expect too much and was mostly satisfied with hearing about Sean.

But by the time I pedaled home, the tension that had eased a bit at Erin's was back. My sweaty clothes stuck to me; I was hot and bothered and short-fused and I found myself shaking as I went into the house, not knowing what to expect.

Dad was barbecuing burgers for dinner. Hannah was still in her room. Everything in the house felt like it was ready to explode, including me.

Dad made Hannah come down to eat, but the two of them didn't say a word to each other. At one point, when they both reached for something at the same time, Hannah jerked her hand back as if she might contaminate herself if she touched Dad.

At that moment, when Dad's eyes glazed and turned away from us, I hated my sister. I almost got up and left. Hannah beat me to it. I managed to force down the rest of my burger before excusing myself, then escaping to my room with my bird books.

Hannah was sitting on the window sill, smoking.

"This is my room," I said, annoyed, and for once, not bothering to hide it.

She shifted farther out the window. "It's not your roof."

I climbed past her, lay back against the warm cedar shakes, closed my eyes and tried to pretend she wasn't there. Instead I felt the heat from the roof moving into my veins; my blood prickled, every nerve in my body felt agitated. The cigarette smoke burned in my nostrils. Hannah's nearness became unbearable.

I thought about leaving and immediately dismissed the notion. This was my place. So I sat up and said shortly, "Can't you go somewhere else?"

"No."

"Go mope in your room or something. This is my space and I don't want you in it."

Hannah didn't move. She butted out her smoke on the roof, flicked it over the edge and said, "I didn't realize I was crowding you. Forgive me."

It wouldn't have mattered what she said. Every word, every movement she made, deliberate and calculated, was fuel. The anger flared in the pit of my stomach. My chest was hot and tight.

"You are unbelievable. Totally unbelievable. You treat everyone around you like scum, you know that? Everyone except your scumbag friends, that is." Somewhere in the back of my mind I kept thinking, Calm down. It's not worth it. But I was past listening.

Hannah just stared straight ahead.

"I don't get it. How could you do those things? Don't you know you're going to get caught? Don't you care? How stupid are you?" Words came spitting out; the fire in my stomach and chest burned out of control. It had been smoldering a long time.

Hannah fired back. "What do you know about it, Kelly? You don't know a thing. You don't even want to know. All you want is for everything to go along nice and quiet and peaceful. Don't bother me and I won't bother you. How can you think that? How can you think life is going to leave you alone like that? Who's the stupid one?"

"Maybe life isn't perfect, but at least I don't go around being an obnoxious brat, making it harder for myself and everyone else."

"No," she snapped. "How could you? As long as you never leave your precious roof you don't have to worry about screwing up, do you? Do you think that's going to keep you from getting hurt? Fat chance. Get a life, loser."

There was a split second of total silence, and then . . .

"Who do you think you are?" I was almost choking on my anger, anger fueled by fear. "If you want to ruin your own life, go ahead. Why do you have to take the rest of us with you? Can't you see what you're doing to Dad?"

Hannah's eyes opened wide, something flashed through them and was gone, her face contorted into a cruel sneer. "What I'm doing to him? That's a good one. How about what he's doing to me? How about what he and Mom have done to me?"

Didn't she know their divorce wasn't about her? "They haven't done anything to you. They didn't split up to hurt you or me. They just split. And we got caught in the crossfire. Period. Grow up and live with it. You don't even give Caryn half a chance."

By now, we were both panting, gulping for air.

"Why should I?" Hannah yelled. "No one has given me half a chance! I don't count for anything! You think you're so perfect, but you're just a hypocrite like everyone else. You don't give a shit about anyone except your precious self. You don't care about me — all you care about is that I don't do anything to spoil your safe little pathetic life!"

"No one can even breathe around this house

because of you! I'm sick of it. I'm sick of you!"

"Not as sick as I am of you." Hannah spoke quietly now, cold and hard and ever so even. "I hate you. All of you." But tears were already brimming in her eyes.

I couldn't stop myself. Even then, when she said what she did, I knew she didn't mean it. They were words uttered in self-defense. But I couldn't stop. I had to defend myself, too. My words were as hard and cold as Hannah's. And I wasn't crying.

"If you hate us so much, why don't you just leave? Good riddance to bad rubbish."

And then she was gone.

I closed my eyes, swallowed painfully. The muscles I'd been holding rigid released and went limp. There was nothing left, nothing but the ashes of my anger and the wound burned deep into my skin by Hannah's words.

Even then, I didn't cry. I looked out over the fields and tentatively probed the rawness. Regret. Guilt. Relief. What else? I didn't know — wasn't sure I *wanted* to know — so I pushed all the feelings away.

The nighthawks were flying low like the night before, just above the pond. I picked up one of my books and flipped through it. There was nothing about nighthawks, not even in the index, which was strange. I grabbed the other hawk book and checked it carefully, almost frantically. Still nothing. Finally I found a listing for nighthawks in the index of the field guide. I flipped to the right page. There it was, in full color. The Common Nighthawk. It was the same bird.

Then I saw the page heading: Goatsuckers.

A nighthawk wasn't a hawk. That's why it wasn't in either of the hawk books. A nighthawk was a species of goatsucker, the same family as whippoorwills.

A goatsucker.

It wasn't right. I started to shiver in the warm night and the burger I'd eaten felt like concrete in the cold pit of my stomach. The words went blurry for a second while I blinked rapidly to clear my eyes. I had to force myself to read what the book said.

Common Nighthawk, Chordeiles minor (Mosquito Hawk, Bull-bat): The most widespread of the six species of goatsuckers found in North America. Goatsuckers are nocturnal insect eaters with large flat heads, small bills, enormous gapes and white patches in wings or tails. Eyes are a mere slit by day, huge and round at night. All except nighthawks are named for their call.

My eyes swimming, I skimmed the words.

. . . The commonly accepted name nighthawk is a misnomer, and probably comes from the bird's likeness to the smaller hawks when observed in flight. In some locations, the bird became known as the bull-bat because of its appearance at dusk, erratic flight resembling that of a bat, and bellowing sound of its courtship dive. It has also been called mosquito hawk, nightjar, will-o'-wisp and pisk . . . Common in open country and cities throughout Canada and the United States, nesting on the ground or rooftops.

There was more, but I barely glanced at it. Nothing was what it was supposed to be anymore. Not even a damn bird. I closed the book and went inside, refusing to look at the birds flying above me.

Lying in bed, I could hear them calling in the night,

a sharp nasal *peent*, just like the book said. I got up and closed the window, then pulled the pillow over my head to shut out the sound and lay there, tossing and turning — until I heard my bedroom window open.

And then I cried.

17

I didn't move at the sound, just opened my eyes enough to watch Hannah disappear into the night. At that moment — in the dark, my heart aching and bruised — part of me hoped she was leaving for good. And another part wanted to grab her and not let her go. But I lay still.

Good riddance to bad rubbish. Remembering my words, overcome with guilt, I got up and peered out the window. She was gone.

I should have told Dad then, but I didn't.

If I hadn't told Hannah to leave, if I'd gone to Dad when she did go, maybe the door bell wouldn't have rung at two o'clock in the morning.

If I hadn't told her to leave, maybe the police

147

wouldn't have brought Hannah home, stoned.

If I hadn't told her to leave —

Maybe we would never have known.

But I did tell her. And so I lay awake in the dark and heard the front door bell ring. I heard Dad answer the door. The murmur of voices. A few clipped words — "river valley . . . bonfire . . . possession . . . hash, uppers." I heard Dad thanking someone. The front door closing. Caryn moving around in the kitchen, making coffee.

A long silence.

The hot summer night was stifling; my room was warm, too warm. But I was shivering when Dad's voice first broke the silence.

"What is it you want, Hannah?" Dad almost cried. "Why are you doing this to yourself?"

Suddenly I was eight years old again, lying awake listening to Mom and Dad fight, willing them to stop. Lying awake long after the voices dropped to a murmur, just in case, knowing, somehow, that if I fell asleep, the voices would start up again.

"Explain yourself." Dad's voice was shaking, barely under control.

There was only silence. I could imagine Hannah sitting there, her eyes dull with dope and alcohol, her face pale, looking at the table, not caring.

"I think I deserve some kind of explanation."

"Do you?" Hannah spoke finally, her words slurred and overly loud. "I can't think of any reason why I should s'plain a thing to you."

Dad ranted about letting her sleep it off and everyone cooling down before they talked about it, but he was too angry to pay any attention to himself.

"I don't know what to do anymore. Tell me, Hannah, what do you want me to do? Just tell me and I'll do it!"

"I want you to go to hell!" Hannah screamed suddenly. "Just go to hell. All of you!" A chair crashed to the ground. There was another horrible silence. I was out of bed now, creeping down the hallway to the top of the stairs.

"Hannah," Caryn said, more quietly. "Try to calm down. Your dad cares about you. We both do. Don't you know that? We're just trying to understand."

"You don't give a damn about me! *You* don't even know me!" Hannah was still shouting. I could hear her panting. "And he's stuck with me, aren't you, *Ian*? You can stop lying. You can tell Mom to stop lying. She stuck you with me, didn't she? Was it some kind of revenge? Boy, you must've really pissed her off. Or maybe — hey, here's a new one I didn't think of before — maybe all this time you kept us to get back at her."

"Hannah," Dad said. The louder Hannah was, the quieter he got. "Come here, kidlet."

"Don't! Don't! Don't!" Hannah screamed again, a wail of despair so deep my knees gave way and I sank to the floor. "Don't pretend anymore! That's all you are, a pretender. A fake. Has it been fun, pretending to be a father?"

"Whatever it is I've done wrong, tell me. Whatever it is you've done, we'll be here for you. Haven't I always been here for you? Talk to me, Hannah. I'm your father. We'll get through this."

"That's just it, *Ian*." Hannah's voice bit with sarcasm. "C'mon. You can tell me. You can admit it."

"What, Hannah? Tell me!"

And she did.

She screamed the words at him. *"YOU'RE NOT MY FATHER, ARE YOU?!"*

The anguish in Hannah's voice tore at my insides. My stomach turned and a bitter lump rose in my throat, burning as I swallowed. Why, why was Hannah doing this? I groaned, suddenly faint as the blood seemed to rush out of my body and leave me cold, my ears ringing. Sitting at the top of the stairs, my arms holding on to the oak spindle of the railing, the world grew distant.

Every breath hurt, every breath squeezed against the throbbing tightness in my chest. She was stoned, she didn't know what she was saying. I waited for Dad to tell her she was crazy. For his voice to push away the dark silence.

But the next voice was Hannah's. Sobbing. Her words were garbled and far away through the strange ringing in my ears. "Don't lie because I know you're not. Your blood type's all wrong. For all I know, Mom's not my mother either. What am I? Adopted? Some kind of test tube baby? Kelly too, or just me? Did you make up all those stories about when I was born? Am I an invention? Am I real? Tell me!! I don't know who I am! When were you going to tell me who I am?!"

There was a loud sob, another crash. The front door slammed. My mouth was dry and tasted like blood.

I didn't realize I was crying until a sob caught in my throat. *Why didn't Dad deny it?*

"Oh, God," Caryn gasped.

"I'm going after her," said Dad. The door slammed again. Somehow, I made it back to my room and closed my door, sobbing, stars breaking everywhere.

In another minute, Caryn was there, knocking on my door. "Kelly? Are you all right? Can I come in?"

She didn't wait for an answer, but came in and sat on the bed. She started to rub her hand up and down my back. I couldn't stand it. I wanted to scream like Hannah.

"I'm okay," I gasped, shuddering. "Please leave me alone."

She stopped and got up. "I'll be here," she said. "I'll be here if you need . . ." Her voice dwindled to a murmur. " . . . anything."

What did Hannah mean? What was happening? I didn't have the courage to ask. Loose threads were hanging everywhere. If I tugged on the wrong one, everything I knew, everything I cared about, everything that made up my life would unravel and disappear. It was disappearing now, coming apart in front of my eyes.

And I didn't know why!

Where were Hannah and Dad? I didn't sleep. I slipped out onto the roof and sat there, wrapped in my housecoat, shivering despite the heat, until I heard them stumble into the house a long time later.

The sky was empty. The stars were hiding behind clouds, the nighthawks sleeping. There was only a faint glow through the shreds of cloud brushing against the moon.

In the darkness, the only sounds were Hannah's sobbing and Dad's voice murmuring evenly. At first I couldn't hear what he was saying, just the soothing rhythm of his voice. Then I recognized a familiar pattern, and the words fell into place.

"On Saturday night I lost my girl, and where do you think I found her? Up in the moon, singing a tune, with all the stars around her."

I listened to him murmuring those words — resurrected from all the nights after Mom left — over and over again. "Up in the moon, singing a tune, with all the stars around her."

Finally, the sobs gave way to a few scattered chokes and then stopped. I heard Dad shut Hannah's door, heard him hesitate outside my door and whisper. "Kelly? Are you awake?" I didn't answer; he went away.

I stayed out in the night for a long time, until morning started to creep over the eastern horizon. Eventually the throbbing pain turned into a dull, empty ache.

When I finally crawled back into my room I took Hannah's softest-ever out of my closet. As quietly as I could, careful not to disturb the fragile silence, I snuck into Hannah's room and tucked her blanket close to her.

Then I went to bed to lie awake the rest of the night, listening.

Wondering.

Why didn't Dad deny it?

Tateby Burke & Kanashiro LAW OFFICE
Barristers and Solicitors

Sharon L. Tateby   Gerald T. Burke   Elaine J. Kanashiro

Ste. 212 Sunalta Building, 523 - 17 Ave. Black Diamond, Alberta T3M 4B8
Tel: (403) 823-1010   Fax: 824-1011

September 1 1998

Ms. Hannah Farrell
562 Willowglen Place
BLACK DIAMOND, Alberta T3P 8B2

Dear Ms. Farrell:

Re: Regina vs. Yourself
      s. 348 Criminal Code and s. 3 Narcotic Control Act

This letter will conclude the matter cited above, following my attendance with
you in Youth Court on August 12 and August 26, 1998.

You will find enclosed a Disposition Report on the sentence you received. I am
pleased we were able to achieve such a satisfactory disposition for you and that
matters have turned out so well. Your Order for Probation outlines specific
conditions which should be read and obeyed with care. If you fail to comply
with the condition of the Probation Order you could, very likely, be charged with
Breach of Probation and find yourself in court on that charge. If you have any
questions in regard to sentencing please do not hesitate to contact me.

I wish you all the best in the future.

Yours truly,

S. Tateby

Sharon Tateby
TATEBY BURKE & KANASHIRO

/el   encs.

18

I was scared to get out of bed in the morning. Scared of what the day would bring. Finally I had to pee so bad I didn't have a choice.

Hannah was in the bathroom, so I slumped against the wall until she came out. She looked at me and tried, but didn't quite manage, to smile. "You look like I feel," she murmured.

"Likewise," I said. Hannah's face was pale and splotchy from crying, her eyes swollen. I took a deep breath. "Hannah, I didn't mean what I said —"

She waved her hand to cut me off. "Save it. Not now." Then she looked at me and added, her voice shaking, "Please?"

I nodded and glanced at Dad and Caryn's open

door. "They're up?"

"Time to hear the big explanation. This should be good."

I hesitated. Hannah sounded so tired. "This is all a joke, isn't it?"

She grimaced. "I just want to get it over with." She turned and went into her room.

I took my time getting showered and dressed before I went downstairs. Hannah was helping herself to a glass of orange juice. Dad and Caryn waited for us. Even though we both dragged our feet doing insignificant tasks — pouring juice, drinking it, rinsing the glass, putting it in the dishwasher, wiping the spill on the counter — eventually there was nothing left to do but sit down at the table.

Hannah launched the first attack. She nodded toward Caryn. "Why is she here?"

Caryn started to get up. "I can leave."

Dad reached over and caught her arm. "No. Please stay." When she hesitated, he repeated, "Please. I want you to stay." Caryn sat back down again and Dad looked at us. "If we are going to be a family, don't we have to start acting like one? I mean, we need to support each other and we can't do that if we don't know what's going on, if we aren't open with each other."

Hannah snorted. "Look who's talking." She was back in form.

Dad flushed. He looked first at Hannah, then me, then Hannah again. He hung his head. "Maybe you're right. I'm not sure how to say this, or even what to say —"

"Let me save you the trouble," Hannah interrupted. "You're not my father. There. Is that what you wanted to say? Is that open enough for you?"

"No, Hannah. That's not what I want to say at all. As far as I'm concerned, in fact, as far as the law is concerned, you are every bit as much my daughter as Kelly. Do you understand?"

"No. I don't." Hannah's voice was barely more than a whisper. Her lip was trembling. "You know that kid's game? Which of these things belongs with the others? Let's see now."

Hannah held up one hand and started counting on her fingers as she talked, her voice getting louder and harder with almost every word. "You have type A blood. Mom has type O, Kelly has type O." She held up one finger on the other hand, staring at it, and quietly said, "And I have type B." She looked straight at Dad, even leaned over the table toward him, menacingly. "You guessed it. I'm the one who doesn't belong. How could that be, you ask? Simple." She stretched out the words, leaving long pauses between each one. Pauses filled with venom. "You're . . . not . . . my . . . father. Isn't science wonderful?"

This was just stupid. "Tell her she's crazy, Dad," I said. "She's gone off the deep end because of some idiotic science fair experiments that aren't even accurate. Those tests —" I was stopped by the look on his face. The way the pain twisted his features and shot through his eyes while he struggled to control it. I recognized the same flash of pain that had come and gone so quickly in Hannah's eyes the day before.

"No. Hannah's not crazy." He took a deep breath and rubbed his forehead. "I don't know if the blood tests you did at the science fair are accurate or not, Hannah. They probably are. It's . . ." He swallowed, fumbling for words, his eyes still searching for a place to settle and then they finally found Hannah, glancing away again. The words eventually came, barely whispered. "It's true that I'm not your biological father."

Hannah blinked, like she hadn't even believed herself. I couldn't take it in. I didn't want to hear it. I stared at the tabletop and listened to the sound of Dad's voice, slow, broken, as if every word hurt.

"Hannah, you've got to believe me. You have been my daughter since the moment you were born, when you woke up screaming at the world around you. I refused to think of you as anything but mine since I held you. I . . . I don't know how to explain —"

"You were there when I was born? I don't understand!" Hannah's voice shook. The anger was all used up and, without it, the anguish of the night before surfaced again. "Who am I?"

"You're Hannah Farrell! Nothing's changed." But Dad's answer was a question, a plea.

"No. Don't tell me that! Who am I really?"

A sigh, almost a whimper, escaped Dad. He ran his hands through his hair, leaving unruly spikes sticking out at odd angles. I wanted to reach across the table and smooth it back for him. "It's the only answer I know, Hannah! For me, that's who you are. Beyond that, who you are, who you want to be — I can't tell you, that's something you have to decide for yourself."

There was a long silence. "If it will help, I'll tell you what happened. It was so long ago, and your mom and I worked so hard at trying to put it behind us."

Hannah grunted. "Tell me." She wasn't going to make this easy on anyone.

Dad lifted his head to glance at us both one more time, but when he started talking he got this weird vacant look in his eyes, as if he was staring at some place far behind us but not really seeing it. "You both know that your mother and I weren't happy together for a long time. Kelly probably doesn't remember, but we had trouble even before Hannah was born. There was so much your mother wanted to do, wanted to be. Kelly came along unexpectedly and having a baby made everything so much more difficult. I was gone most of the time, working. She was confused. I didn't understand. We separated for a while. All the reasons don't matter now."

"You separated?" I didn't know anything about that part of my parents' story. Caryn reached over and held Dad's hand. He blinked and came part way back to us.

"You were only two years old, Kelly. You and Mom lived in an apartment for about eight months before we worked things out and you both came home."

I couldn't believe it. I had no memory of anything like that.

"Go on," Hannah said.

"We discovered she was pregnant shortly after we got back together."

Tears trickled down Hannah's face. "So it was the milkman all along."

"Please, Hannah. Try to understand. It wasn't like that. Not at all. When Maddie told me, I was deva-stated. So was she. But . . . well, we both saw other people while we were separated. Sometimes things don't go as expected."

This was more than I wanted to know about my parents. And Dad wasn't finished yet.

"We didn't know what to do. Despite all our prob-lems, we did care for each other. We still do. We just wanted such different things out of life."

"Why didn't she get an abortion?" Hannah was shaking now. Her whole body was trembling. She clasped her hands together on the table.

"I won't lie to you, Hannah. We did consider it. But we both wanted another child some time, if not right then. The doctor warned us that abortion always carried the risk of an infection that could make having another child difficult. But even without the warn-ing . . . well, when the time came to make the decision, neither of us could do it. I guess, in the end, we ran out of time."

Hannah closed her eyes, whispered, "And then along came Hannah."

Dad reached out and put his big rough hand over both Hannah's white shaking hands. His fingers wrapped themselves around hers and held them still. "We never regretted it, even after we couldn't hold our marriage together."

I was completely stunned. Hannah, not my sister? I couldn't begin to imagine what Hannah was feeling. She sat there for a few seconds, then slowly pulled her hands out of Dad's. She looked up with this lost, bewildered expression on her face. Her eyes found mine.

And I looked away.

Because at that moment, the thing I felt most was relief, relief that I wasn't Hannah. That my father was still my father. That I knew who I was. At least I thought I did, maybe for the last time in my life.

Hannah stared at her lap, the tears running in a steady stream down her cheeks.

Dad kept talking, softly now. I felt like his voice, his words, were the only things holding us up. "Hannah, I've always thought you came from the best of what your mother and I had to give each other. That's the thought I hung on to, at first, when we were struggling with the whole idea, and then I didn't need that thought anymore. I had you."

Hannah wasn't buying it. "Who's my biological father?" She spoke to her lap.

"As far as the law is concerned, Hannah, I am your father," Dad said. "We were married, I'm your legal father. It's as simple as that." He didn't sound like he convinced even himself. This time things couldn't be that straightforward.

Now Hannah stared at him, her face chiseled again under the streaks of tears. "No, it's not. As far as I'm concerned, I want to know who my real father is."

Dad closed his eyes briefly. When he opened them he didn't waver, but looked straight at Hannah. "I never knew . . . I . . . I didn't want to know. If you feel you must, you'll have to talk to your mother. I'll call her and explain. You should talk to her anyway."

Hannah nodded ever so slightly. She was so pale I wondered how she managed to keep from collapsing. "Okay. When I'm ready."

Dad looked done in. "I can understand why you're angry, Hannah. I'm sorry for how hurt you must feel. We didn't mean for you to be hurt. Maybe we made a mistake, but we really didn't see any reason why you should ever know. We didn't want to put you through what you must be going through now. I'm . . . I'm just so sorry, kidlet."

Hannah's tears were falling again, silently. I could barely hear what she was saying as she struggled to keep control. "How . . . how could you love someone else's baby? How am I supposed to believe that?" She cried out, lifting her eyes to Dad's, "How can you even stand the sight of me?"

Dad was crying now, too, and shaking his head. "Hannah, I can't explain how it happened. I don't know . . . when you were born I was afraid to touch you. I was afraid of what I would feel. But then I held you, and it was incredible what happened. I was so surprised, but what I felt was the same wonder and pride and . . . and overwhelming awe that I felt when I first held Kelly. I didn't understand either, and the feeling was altogether too amazing and fragile to question. I was just so thankful. After a while, I hardly remembered that you weren't mine. It wasn't even an issue when your mom and I divorced.

"It's okay if you find it hard to understand. If I have to prove it to you every day for the rest of my life, I will. You can be as angry as you like, but I'll always be your father. I won't ever leave you, Hannah. I will always love you, whatever happens."

I believed him. Not just because I wanted to, but because I knew my father. When he said he would do something, he did it.

But I wasn't Hannah.

"You're leaving to go back to B.C. after court tomorrow, aren't you?" Hannah's voice was such a mixture of bitterness and despair. She wiped her face on the sleeve of her sweatshirt.

She was right. He was leaving us again.

Just like Mom was always leaving us.

"No," Dad said. "I'm not going back. No job is that important. If I had known — well, if I had known, I never would've taken the job in the first place. It doesn't matter now. I'm staying here."

My heart skipped a little. As long as Dad was here, things would somehow work out. In the middle of all the muddle and heartache, I still believed that. I wanted, I needed to have him close for awhile, available, to figure out how I felt about this person who was my father, who had done what he had done. And Mom. Somehow I was going to have to face Mom.

If I needed him, how much more would Hannah? But I should have known better.

"I think you should go," Hannah said, barely hesitating. "The job's almost over, isn't it? I think you should go. It would give me time to decide for myself how I feel and what I should do. I just want to be left alone."

No, I cried to myself. Alone isn't any good!

But I had already lost the right to tell her what I thought.

Dad's grey eyes were soft. He nodded. "We have another day until your court appearance. It's up to you, but I want you to be very sure about this."

Two little words would have been enough. All Hannah had to say was, "Please stay." I couldn't understand when she didn't. Not until later did I figure out that there was just too much in the way for the words to come through. And there was something else, too. Some deep terrible need to strike back.

"I'll think about it," she said. "But you should probably go."

And that was that. Somehow we muddled through the rest of the day. Hannah's lawyer went to court with her the next day. We were all there. Dad managed to reach Mom. They talked on the phone for a long time, and she flew back from Vancouver to be there too.

Hannah pleaded guilty. The prosecution said Hannah refused to tell the police who was with her, that she lied to them, that there were already additional charges pending. Hannah's lawyer argued that it was Hannah's first offence, that she was a good student who got mixed up with the wrong crowd and was intimidated by them, that she had the support of her parents who were with her in court, that she showed genuine remorse for her actions.

I thought the judge might have a hard time believing that last part, the way Hannah was staring icily into space. But how else was she supposed to hold herself together? The judge looked at her hard for a long time after the lawyers had finished talking.

Then he ordered a predisposition report and delayed sentencing for two weeks. Hannah was released into Dad's custody.

Outside the courthouse, Mom tried to talk to Hannah. "I guess you have a lot of questions," she said, putting her arm around Hannah's shoulder.

Hannah shrugged her arm off. "Yeah, but why would I expect to get honest answers?" She looked straight at Mom. She was shaking. "Do you even remember the guy's name?" She turned away and went straight to the car, leaving Mom standing there, stunned.

Dad touched Mom's arm lightly. "We're going to have to give her some time."

She nodded silently.

Because of the judge's order, the probation officer came to our house. He talked to Dad and Caryn and me. He talked to Hannah. He talked to Mom. He even talked to the principal at Hannah's school.

Hannah didn't change her mind. She still wanted Dad to go back to B.C. At least that's what she insisted she wanted.

So he did.

Maybe he was wrong to leave, maybe Hannah was just testing him and he failed again. What did she expect? He didn't have any fight left in him. Hannah had won.

Mom kept phoning and wanting to see Hannah, but she kept refusing.

I met Mom for dinner once, but I wasn't ready to talk to her about the whole thing yet, either. Even listening to her stumbling through her version was more than I could take. I told her I had a headache, and left the restaurant early.

Funnily enough, Caryn turned out to be the one who was safe to be around during what I've come to think of as our recovery time. She didn't push us or say anything when I spent most of my time at home in my darkroom, and Hannah took to sitting on the roof outside my window.

I developed the photos from our holiday. The photo of Hannah pulling herself out of the icy pool turned out so well I enlarged it. She was grinning, and her eyes were bright. The tattoo showed clearly. Funny how I never noticed it when I took the picture. I pinned the photo to the wall in the darkroom.

Two weeks later, Dad flew back for the day and we were all in court again where Hannah had to face a possession charge on top of the break-and-enter. She quietly pleaded guilty a second time.

She was given a year's probation with the condition that she attend school, and a ten o'clock curfew unless she was in the company of her parents or other responsible adults, along with mega community service hours.

She also got a lecture from the judge. "The next time I see you in my courtroom, you will be looking at a custody sentence," he told her.

But it was all over now, I thought, walking out of court that day. There couldn't possibly be a next time.

Hannah,

Can you get out tonight? You're not going to let a stupid curfew get in your way of a good time, are you?

David and Jason and the gang are getting a keg. All you need is $20 to throw into a pot. Just a couple of discs. I'll get the guys to pick you up, usual place. Eleven. Be there.

It's Friday, babe! Time to par-tee!

Nat

Hans,

You are too, too much!
Smooth as silk. The
way you looked Findlay
in the face and told
him he could go to
hell for all you cared.

What did Potvin say?
I can't believe you're
back in class. I thought
you were out on your
ass for sure. Bet
you wish you were.
Who needs it!

Nat

19

I was glad when school started the following week. It gave me something to think about besides home, and since no one there knew what was going on (at least not the family part; everyone knew everything about Hannah going to court) it gave me some space in which to breathe. That was how it felt to me.

I thought it would be that way for Hannah, too. We didn't talk much. I think we didn't know what to say to each other. I spent a lot of time running, and fiddling around in my darkroom. But nothing was the same.

It was easy, too easy, to simply not join the photo club, to turn down Sean when he cornered me at school about the cross-country team. I let everyone think I was upset about Hannah and that things at home were too difficult right now for me to care about anything else. It was all true, just not for the reasons people believed. The gossip was a welcome diversion.

Even Erin attributed my quiet retreat to Hannah's arrest. I let her think what she wanted. The truth was too horrible to share, even with her.

I was still trying to figure out how I felt about Dad's story. I knew the equilibrium in my family had been turned upside-down and sideways. Even though she'd broken the law, it was Hannah who suddenly held all the power. I was scared of what she might decide to do with it.

Mostly, I guess, I was scared of Hannah.

Dad called almost every night. Hannah spoke to him in monosyllables — when she consented to speak to him at all. I wasn't all that talkative, either. It's hard to remember — those weeks passed in such a muffled fog. Every phone call seemed to take Dad further away from us.

Every so often, when Hannah let her guard down for a second, there would be this abandoned, empty look on her face that ripped right through me. I admired the way she managed to get through each day. But even then, when I wanted to reach out to her, to offer some support, I found myself backing away instead. The best I could manage was to keep her company out on the roof once in a while. We rarely saw the nighthawks anymore.

Hannah didn't exactly encourage contact, either. She went to school; after school, she went to the nursing home for a couple of hours. She managed to get assigned to Marge again. Somehow it made me feel better, thinking of Hannah playing checkers with Mr. Fletcher.

In the evenings, she usually stayed home and did homework in her room or watched TV. Twice a week she went to see a family counselor, only because Dad insisted on it before he would go back to B.C.

At home, when she talked at all, she talked about ordinary, everyday things. She spent hours out on the driveway with her basketball, practicing. I watched her through the window one day, taking shot after shot. Moving deliberately, methodically. Twenty-five free throws, twenty-five from the top of the key, twenty-five from along the baseline, twenty-five lay-ups . . . twenty-five free throws.

I couldn't remember the last time Hannah had laughed.

Every movement she made gave the impression that to move at all was an effort, that every action and word was forced, as if she could barely scrape up enough energy to maintain appearances.

What would she do, I wondered one day, if the effort became too much? I started to watch her, closely.

And as soon as I did, I noticed that Caryn was watching her, too.

Then a couple of weeks after school started, Kyle showed up at the house. He looked relieved to see me when I answered the door. "Hey, Kelly. Is Hannah around?"

I hadn't seen Kyle since spring. He was taller than Hannah now. With his summer tan and longer hair, he seemed a lot older, while Hannah seemed younger than ever.

"She'll be home soon. She spends some time at the nursing home after school," I explained vaguely, not sure what he knew.

"Yeah. She told me. That's why I came by now — I wanted to talk to you when she wasn't here." With his hands in his pockets and shuffling one foot back and forth across the porch, Kyle suddenly turned into a kid again.

"Do you want to come in?"

"No, thanks. I have to go right away. Soccer practice. I was just wondering about Hannah."

There was something he wasn't saying. "Is something wrong at school?"

"Not really. She and Findlay butted heads one day and she got kicked out of class, but nothing serious." Kyle glanced into the house behind me. I got the idea and stepped outside, closing the door.

"Look, Kelly," he said. "I can see why Hannah acts like she does, pretending it's no big deal to get arrested and everything. I wouldn't like everyone staring at me, either."

Hannah must be doing a pretty good job of playing the part, I thought. Kyle didn't know the half of what she was hiding. Maybe there was something I could do for Hannah. "Kyle, there's something else. At home here, I mean. I don't think I should tell you. Maybe Hannah will eventually. But if there's anything you can do at school to help her out . . ." My words trailed off. She could use a friend, I was going to say.

Kyle nodded. "I thought maybe there was some-thing more."

I looked at him, curious. What did he know? "Did Hannah say something?" I asked him.

"No, not really. Not at first. But . . ." He looked away, clearly embarrassed. "Remember when I was telling you about the science fair, when Hannah pushed me? I thought about it a lot, after that, and well, I thought maybe the science fair had something to do with things."

I sat down slowly. "Yes," I said. "I suppose it does."

He hesitated; I told him to go on.

"See, I remembered your blood types. And Hannah's, from when we practiced the procedure at home. I figured Hannah made such a scene because she wanted to distract me. Because she didn't want to do her blood type again, just after your mom and dad had done theirs. She was hoping I wouldn't remember hers, that I wouldn't figure things out. But I have a good memory."

"How long have you known?"

"Pretty much since that day."

"We didn't know," I said slowly, "until a few weeks ago. Hannah and Dad — she's not really saying much to any of us right now."

"She made me promise not to tell," Kyle mumbled. "She wouldn't have anything to do with me for a long time. When I finally got her to talk to me, she made me promise to stay out of it. I wanted her to talk to your dad, but she said she couldn't just yet. I was scared, if I said anything, she'd shut me out again."

"You were probably right."

"She knows I'm on her side. Once or twice lately, I almost thought she wanted to talk about something, but then she just clams up. I've been happy that she wants me around. I don't want to push my luck."

"What about Amy?"

He shrugged. "That's all over."

"Sorry," I said.

"Yeah, well, I wouldn't be here today, except . . . it's like this. I've been keeping an eye on Hannah, you know. Because she's scaring me a little."

Kyle, too.

"Anyway, I've seen her trying to avoid Natalie and the rest of them. Really trying. But they're not going to let her, Kel. Yesterday, I saw Natalie and one of her friends follow her into the girls' washroom. They came out again almost right away, but Hannah didn't come out for a long time after. Not until the bell rang for class. She was late of course and got into more trouble."

My stomach whined. "What do you think happened?"

"I don't know. It's not like there's anything to report to the police and even if there was, I'm not sure it would do any good. When I asked her about it she just told me it was her problem. I thought maybe you'd have an idea about what to do."

Kyle sat beside me. It was almost a relief, to be talking to someone without having to hide the horrible secret. I trusted him. He'd known all along, hadn't he, before we did, and he hadn't betrayed Hannah.

But Kyle was asking me to make a clear-cut choice. Was I going to stay away from Hannah's mess, or step in it?

"I don't know, Kyle. Hannah doesn't exactly tell me anything, either."

"Isn't there something you can do?"

And that's when I remembered Hannah's box. I had a feeling the box could probably tell me something about what was going on. If I wanted to find out. Did I?

"I suppose I have an idea that might work," I said vaguely. "I'm not sure, though."

Kyle stood up. "Okay. I'll stay close to her at school in the meantime. You'll call me?"

Reluctantly, I said that I would.

H,

Hey don't worry. They can't do anything to you in baby court. What's the worst that can happen? More community house - You like those old folks, don't you?

Besides, no way anything can happen. You can't back out on us now, girl!

N

H—

Your stepwitch won't let me talk to you on the phone. You say you can't sneak out (what happened to the escape route?), you take off as soon as the bell rings every day. How are we supposed to get together? We've got things to talk about.

Look. D says we have to be there tonight. I don't know what he might do if you don't show up. You've got to find a way.

If you are any kind of friend, you'll make it!

N

20

Even after dawdling at the library after school the next day, I was still the first one home. There was a note on the kitchen counter from Caryn. She was catering some business reception, but would be back for dinner.

The house was empty.

I climbed the stairs a little nervously, and pushed open the door to Hannah's room. My palms were sweating and I was shaking. I told myself that what I was doing was wrong, invading Hannah's privacy, but even then I knew I wasn't worried about that so much as just plain scared of what I might find.

Hannah's room was a disaster area, like always, but I knew what I was looking for. I kicked a pile of clothes to one side and stretched out on my back on the floor beside her bed. I reached up under the box spring.

The box was there, wedged in the space between the heavy springs and the wooden slats, right where I knew it would be. She'd either forgotten I saw her hiding it that day, or she wanted me to find it.

When I pulled out the box, something heavy slid around on the bottom.

There I sat, cross-legged on the floor of Hannah's room, surrounded by her mess, staring at her box of secrets. The box had once held a pair of hiking boots, so it was fairly big. On the outside, Hannah had used a red felt marker to scribble, "HANDS OFF! Don't even think about it!"

I opened it and fingered through the contents. There didn't seem to be any order to the papers and other stuff. There were a lot of notes on scraps of looseleaf folded into tiny squares. Among the notes were thin, yellow, official looking documents, postcards, school papers, letters, sports day ribbons, a homemade potholder, a bunch of cards, the odd photo, even a dried-up pink rose I recognized. We wore pink roses at Dad and Caryn's wedding.

I recognized the diary I gave Hannah three Christmases ago. It looked brand new and it wasn't locked. I opened it.

"Dear Diary," Hannah had written on the first page, "I don't like diaries. Better luck next time. Bye." The rest of the pages were blank, a few of them torn out.

Hannah was more of a scavenger than a journal writer, I guess. She kept junk. Or maybe it wasn't all junk. I remembered when she made the potholder —

she was only seven or eight. She spent an entire Saturday afternoon weaving it out of scraps of wool like she learned in school. She was going to give it to Mom for Mother's Day, but she obviously didn't.

The box tilted on my lap and the heavy object slid along the bottom again. Holding my breath, I reached through the papers.

My fingers touched something cold and hard. I pulled out an ordinary table knife, its blade scorched an oily bronzy blue. And then I noticed the little plastic bags. Two of them.

One contained a dark tarry lump. The other held eight small pills.

I was vibrating. My heart was racing. I didn't really think, I just scooped up the plastic bags and flushed their contents down the toilet. Watching the drugs swirl around in the toilet bowl made me queasy, so I went to the sink and splashed some water on my face. Drugs just weren't part of my world. My world was ordered and reasoned and . . . safe. But my world was rapidly coming apart.

With the toilet flushing and the water running, I hadn't heard the door opening downstairs.

"What are you doing?"

At first I panicked at the sound of Hannah's voice, froze with the towel held up to my face. Then, I think, I was almost relieved. I finished drying my face and turned around. Hannah was staring at me, not glaring or fuming, just staring with that vacant look in her eyes.

"You were in my box," she said. A flat statement,

with no hint of anger. This Hannah was almost more frightening than the angry Hannah.

"Yes." I took a deep breath and added, "I flushed the drugs."

Hannah smirked. "No shit, Sherlock. I was going to anyway." She turned and walked into her room without another word, closing the door behind her.

And I stood there, aching, not for myself this time, but for Hannah. I stood there for a long time, without a clue what to do, only knowing that I had to do something.

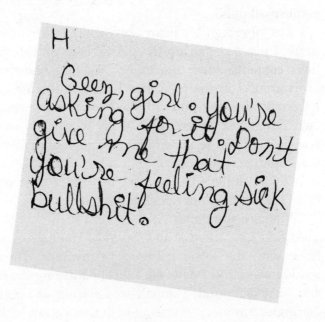

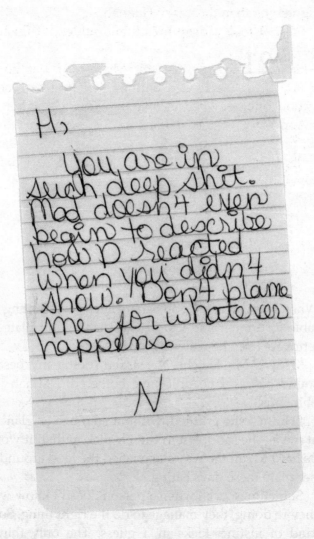

H,

You are in such deep shit. Mad doesn4 even begin to describe how I reacted when you didn4 show. Don4 blame me for whatever happens.

N

21

When Hannah came downstairs later, I was setting the table for dinner and Caryn was dishing out plates of leftovers from her catering job.

"How's Mr. Fletcher?" I asked, doing my best to sound casual. I needn't have bothered. Hannah was oblivious.

"Hmm," she grunted, without so much as glancing at me as she sat down to eat. Or pick, rather. It would be hard to call the way she pushed the food around on her plate these days eating.

Sometimes, even when a person doesn't know what they're doing, they manage to do the right thing. Some kind of instinct kicks in, I guess. The only thing I could think of to get Hannah's attention and finish what I had started was to get in her face. So I stared at her. Eventually she put her fork down and looked back at me.

"What?"

Good question. I had her attention; now what was I supposed do? I felt like I was going to choke, but I also desperately wanted to connect with my sister in some way. Any way. "Nothing. You want some milk?" Her eyes followed me as I went to the fridge for the milk and filled two glasses. I put one down in front of Hannah.

"You don't have to be nice to me."

I sighed. "Okay, I won't then." I took Hannah's glass, poured the milk back into the carton and sat down. Hannah looked at me and shook her head. She reached for the carton and refilled her glass. Then she raised her glass in a silent toast.

I lifted my glass back at her. "Hey," I answered, relaxing a little. Caryn, I noticed, was watching us curiously. Good luck figuring it out, I thought. I sure didn't know what I was doing.

But it seemed to have worked, whatever it was. After dinner I casually mentioned that I thought I'd go for a walk, and turned to Hannah. "Do you want to come along?"

"That's a great idea, Kelly," Caryn said, smoothing the way. I was grateful to her. "It's a beautiful evening. Hannah, why don't you join her? I'll clean up here."

Hannah shrugged, not appearing to care one way or the other. "Yeah. Okay."

The evening was warm and comfortable. We walked

along the back alley behind our place and watched the sun settle over the empty field. All that remained after the harvest was stubble. A few pheasants were making their way through the field, picking at leftovers.

We walked in silence, along the back alley to the pond at the end of the field. The understanding between us was still too tentative for words. It was enough, for now, to be there together.

On our way back, as we approached the house, a shadowy form suddenly fluttered up from the alley. We stopped short as the bird came directly at us, veering off to one side almost in front of my face.

We stood quietly — our faces turned to the sky — and the nighthawk came back.

It danced for us, then.

Not the daring, swooping dives of before, but a teasing, playful dance, as if the bird was reveling in the sheer joy of its ability to move through the air. It swooped toward us, circled back, turned skyward to glide silently above us. Around and around it leaped and twirled, its earthy brown feathers brilliantly bronze in the warm golden spotlight of the setting sun.

The bird was so close. I imagined I could see each feather, sharp and distinct. The broad white bars on its wings flashed as the nighthawk turned and twisted. In the sky above us, for one brief moment the sun hesitated, cradled on the horizon. Wings whispered a last blessing, and were gone.

I don't know how long we stood there. Probably no more than a minute or two. When I think about it, I suppose the bird was simply checking us out, because we were too close to its space or something.

But the bird's flight felt more like a prayer than anything else. A kind of forgiveness.

"It's saying good-bye," I whispered, when I was able to catch my breath.

Hannah nodded. "Winter's coming. Ian will be home soon."

She opened her mouth again, as if she wanted to say something else. Then she turned back to the house and my heart tore away from the bird in the sky to follow her.

"Hannah, I want to help. What can I do to help?"

"You can't."

"Maybe not. But I will if I can. If it's not too late. I've been thinking a lot about things and this is what I came up with." I paused, licked my lips. I hadn't planned this. I was just feeling my way, and it was harder than I'd ever imagined. The words needed to be right.

"If it was me this had happened to, I don't think I could've handled it. I . . . I think you're stronger than me."

"Is that what it looks like? Like I'm strong?"

"Yeah. Look, Hannah, I don't know who you are, either. I don't even know who I am anymore. But I know that you're a part of who I am. And we're a part of you, I think. Dad, Mom and me. Caryn, too. Kyle. All of us are part of you. You can't discard us like old clothes. We'll always be a part of your life. And you'll be a part of ours. Nothing can change that."

Hannah was staring out over the field.

"I'm really sorry I said those awful things that

night," I added quietly.

I wasn't sure Hannah had heard me. She continued to stare into the distance. "After the science fair, I started calling him Ian. It didn't hurt so much to think of him as Ian. I always felt like I didn't belong somehow — I wasn't like Dad or Mom. I sure wasn't like you. And I finally knew why."

I held my breath and listened.

"I invented all kinds of revenge. I'd run away, I'd disappear in the night. I wanted to hurt him. I wanted to hurt him before he could hurt me anymore. Because if he wasn't my father, I figured eventually he was going to leave, too. Like Mom. But this time I would be ready. I would leave first."

"Why didn't you?"

"I don't know. I felt . . . naked, I guess, like I had nothing to protect me anymore. I wanted to hide somewhere, where no one could find me. Lots of mornings, I would look in the mirror and see this person called Hannah Farrell — it wasn't me because I knew I wasn't Hannah Farrell, right? And since my life was all a fake, all bogus anyway, I could make Hannah Farrell be anybody I wanted to be. I didn't matter."

"Your life isn't bogus."

The corners of Hannah's mouth lifted a little, but you couldn't really call it a smile. "I invented a new me, and that was my hiding place. You have your roof, and I had this new me, who liked to get wasted, because then the little bit of the old me left inside disappeared completely and nothing could touch me."

"And now?" I almost whispered the question.

She shrugged. "Maybe the person I invented is the real me. I don't know. But I know being wasted doesn't work. You just wake up hurting more than ever . . . Don't worry. I figured that much out." Hannah's voice was bitter again. "See what you can learn in therapy? But they can't tell me who I am, either."

She turned and walked back into the house.

Watching her walk away, I felt totally drained. The last thing I wanted to do was talk to Kyle or anybody else right then. So I was a little re-lieved when no one answered the phone at his place.

When Kyle and I checked in with each other a few days later, I found out what had happened to him that day outside the school, and why he'd got home late. Some driver, drunk probably, jumped the curb and came close to running him over. Kyle was okay, thank goodness. We agreed that, as far as Hannah was concerned, all we could do was stay close to her, and wait until she was ready to talk to us.

It never occurred to either of us to connect his accident with what was happening to Hannah.

Youth has close call with reckless driver

Police are looking for the driver of a car that narrowly missed hitting a student in front of Willow Park Middle School last night.

Kyle Hirano was leaving the school after a soccer game when a dark green four-door car veered off the road and on to the sidewalk where he was waiting at a bus stop. Hirano said he saw the car coming in time to jump out of its way.

"I heard this thunk when the car jumped the curb, and looked up to see it headed right at me. I didn't have time to think, I just jumped back behind the bus stop sign. The car glanced off the pole, back on to the street and took off."

Hirano escaped with a twisted ankle and a bruised elbow from falling on the sidewalk in his hurry to get out of the car's path.

Police are looking for the driver of a dark green Ford with damage to the right fender. Anyone with information is asked to call Crime Stoppers at 823-7867.

HANNAH,

I'M FINE. I WAS FRIGTENED MORE THAN ANYTHING ELSE. MY ANKLE IS PERFECTLY FINE. JUST A MINOR SPRAIN. I WON'T EVEN MISS SOCCER PRACTISE.

BUT WHY IS NATALIE ASKING ME ALL KINDS OF QUESTIONS ABOUT ~~ARE~~ YOU? I HOPE IT'S BECAUSE YOU'RE NOT TALKING TO HER.

MAYBE I COULD COME OVER AND WE COULD PLAY SOME BBALL AGAIN SOMETIME? ARE YOU GOING TO TRY OUT FOR THE TEAM?

KYLE

22

One minute I was laughing, scooping gooey, stringy mush out of the pumpkin Caryn had finally picked out after checking every available pumpkin at the Farmers' Market.

"This is your brain." I held up the pumpkin in one hand and with the other shoved the spoonful of pumpkin guts into Hannah's face. "This is your brain on drugs."

Hannah wrinkled her nose and scowled. She shoved my hand away. "Get a life, Kelly." But she was smiling.

Some of the mess ended up on the floor. "Gee thanks, Hannah. Now clean it up."

"Yeah, right." She took the lid I had carved out of the top of the pumpkin and started spinning it on the counter.

I grinned at her. It felt so good at that moment to have our relationship resemble something normal. I thought I detected signs that Hannah was beginning to show an interest in life again.

And I was surprising myself by having fun helping Caryn get ready for Thanksgiving weekend. There were fresh cinnamon buns cooling on the counter, and an apple crisp in the oven. The kitchen was filled with a spicy warmth that drifted through the rest of the house. Even the laughter coming from the TV seemed to fit.

A good part of my contented mood, I knew, was because Dad was coming home tonight, or tomorrow at the latest — finally. He would take care of things. Somehow. I would try to get Hannah to tell him about getting hassled at school. But if she refused, I was going to do it, no matter how mad it made her.

I grabbed some paper towels and wiped up the mess myself. If I waited for Hannah to clean it up, the stuff would dry there and stick to the lino. Even if Caryn was being easy on Hannah these days, I wasn't going to risk starting an argument tonight.

I scooped more pumpkin guts onto the wax paper. "Now I've just got to pick out the seeds."

"Why do you bother?" Hannah picked up a fork and poked a flat pumpkin seed out of the stringy mess. She nibbled on it carefully. "Totally tasteless."

"Toasted. Caryn is going to toast them with something or other. She says they will be a quote, culinary delight, unquote."

I started poking the seeds away from the pulp. "Besides, it's not a bother." I was learning that I could actually enjoy doing things with Caryn, once I figured out that her kind of fun wasn't the same as Mom's. I smiled to myself, wondering briefly what Mom was doing for Thanksgiving in New Orleans. Did they make cajun turkey?

I made a tentative attempt to gauge Hannah's mood. "We're starting a new family tradition." Even I could hear how matter-of-fact I sounded, just like Dad.

Hannah shrugged. "Okay. The house does smell nice," she conceded for once. She sauntered over and curled up in the overstuffed armchair in the family room next to the kitchen nook.

Encouraged, I ventured further. "Hey, don't basketball tryouts start soon? You're going out for the team, aren't you?"

Hannah looked thoughtful, almost teasing. Then, like only she could do, she caught me totally off guard. "Tell you what, Kel. I'll play basketball this year, if you join the cross-country team."

I sputtered. "What?"

She nodded at the fridge where we posted phone messages. "The coach called while you were out buying groceries. Wants to know if you can substitute at their next meet for someone who's injured. Sounded like he would be awfully grateful to have the fabled Kelly Farrell, who he's heard so much about, on his team. Seems someone named Sean has been telling him how great you are."

I blushed and read the message. There was a phone number to call.

"Well?" Hannah said. "What excuse can you come

up with to get out of this one?"

She was testing me. I was determined not to fail. Not now. "You're on," I said. My mouth suddenly dry, I took the message over to the phone and dialed the number. When I hung up, after promising to be at practice next week, Hannah looked as surprised as I felt.

"All right, Kelly!" she said softly. Then she grinned. "I was going to play basketball anyway."

I let it be. I knew better than to push too far. The worst seemed to be over, but I was still a little wary of saying something that would open the wounds again. Besides, I could always quit the team after the meet if I didn't like it.

Caryn walked in with a pile of freshly laundered dish towels. She looked around for a clean surface to put them on and finally settled on Hannah's lap. "How would you like to fold these and put them away for me, Hannah?"

"How would I like to?" Hannah repeated. "Friday night. I'm stuck at home because nobody even goes out until nine and I have a ten o'clock curfew — and you ask me how would I like to fold laundry?"

"Let me rephrase that," Caryn said. "Please fold these and put them away for me."

Hannah grinned. "I'll get right on it, Herr Commandant, seeing as how I'm confined to quarters anyway."

Caryn didn't bite. "That's Frau Commandant."

She was learning. I had to give her that. The two of them seemed to be getting along a little better, in an odd sort of head-butting way. Hannah was almost cheerful.

Then it hit me. Little sister was looking forward to

having Dad home, too.

Maybe things would be okay after all. Not right away, maybe, but eventually.

And the next minute the phone rang.

23

The phone rang a second time.

That's all it took for the warm, safe feeling — all feeling — to shatter completely. Time was suddenly smashed into smithereens: sharply focused fragments with jagged, cutting edges.

The first fragment broke away as Hannah pounced on the receiver.

"Yo!" she said. Caryn rolled her eyes at me and I smiled.

Hannah held out the phone. "They want to speak to Mrs. Farrell." She sounded curious.

Caryn took the receiver. She looked at Hannah suspiciously, then gestured to her to turn down the volume on the TV. With the sound muted, I could hear the rain tap-tapping on the windows. If it got much colder, the streets would be covered in ice by morning.

"Hello, this is Caryn Farrell." Caryn was still watching Hannah keenly. Hannah just leaned over the counter and shrugged her shoulders with wide-open eyes as if to say, "Don't look at me!"

Then Caryn's face lost its color and the suspicious look in her eyes was disintegrated by a flash of fear. She swayed a bit, steadying herself against the armchair.

"Yes. Okay," Caryn almost whispered. "Thank you." She hung up, both hands clenching the receiver.

"What?" asked Hannah. "What is it? I didn't do anything, honest!"

There was Hannah, sprawled over the armchair. There was me, standing in front of a mess of pumpkin schlop. There was Caryn, her hand on the phone, staring past us both. Looking right through us. She took a deep breath; I watched her chest and shoulders move.

"What's wrong?" Hannah asked again, less sure of herself this time.

Caryn remembered we were there. "Oh. Kelly, Hannah. Get your things."

Hannah and I looked at each other. What things? I thought.

Caryn started to move. "Ian — your dad — he was in a bad accident coming through the pass. They're bringing him into the hospital by helicopter."

The first cut sliced deep. A splinter of time embedded forever.

I swallowed. My mouth was suddenly dry. "Is he okay?" I asked. "Is he going to be okay?" We were all moving now, down the hall. We grabbed jackets out of the closet.

"He's badly hurt. That's what they said, 'He's badly hurt.'" Caryn was having trouble getting the words out. Her eyes were a little wild. She patted her jacket pocket, felt the top of the hall table. "My keys. God, where are my keys?"

She grabbed her purse and rummaged through it until she found her car keys.

"Okay. Let's go." She dashed out to the garage. Hannah stood in the hallway, holding her jacket, dazed.

"C'mon!" I grabbed her arm and she stumbled along behind me.

I had to remind Caryn to close the garage door as we pulled out into the street. The car tires squealed a little on the wet pavement as we drove off. I looked back.

The house lights burned bright along a jagged edge.

Fragments exploded everywhere, one precisely etched moment after another.

At the hospital. They wouldn't let us see him. He was unconscious, they said, and going into surgery even as they spoke. They said he was bleeding internally, and was very weak. They said it was going to take a while. They said to wait, and to pray.

They said it didn't look good.

Caryn looked at us and desperately reached for our hands. The three of us stood there awkwardly, holding onto each other from a distance. Fragmented.

Hannah was the first to pull away. She backed off, shaking her head. "No, no," she whispered. "He promised." The words were a hoarse, broken plea. She kept shaking her head, and backing away.

Softly, ever so softly, Caryn said, "Hannah." Her name settled over us.

Hannah moaned. "I'm going to be sick." She ran down the hall and across the foyer. The automatic doors opened. The night on the other side was waiting for her. She ran into the dark. A fragment splashed with rain.

I swallowed the sweet saliva flooding into my mouth and whirled around to look at Caryn. She sank down into one of the chairs in the hallway and sobbed. I whirled back. Hannah was gone. There was a weird, distant ringing in my ears.

"I'll go." I choked on the words.

I strode across the foyer, faster and faster, paused while the doors opened for me, peered through the falling rain. A shadow, darker than the rest, was crossing the parking lot. The figure passed under the flood of a streetlight before disappearing again.

I ran, following the movement ahead. My feet slapped the pavement and then sank into the wet grass and I kept running. There were lights behind and ahead, but the expanse of lawn was dark and slick. The shadow that was Hannah had disappeared. I heard a noise, turned and slipped, falling on my knees, hard. I crawled toward the sound. Cold soaked through my jeans.

Hannah was on her knees, heaving and retching on the grass. I held her wet hair back from her face. Her hand squeezed my arm tight. I pulled her away from the mess on the lawn, resisting the impulse to gag.

When she was done, I lifted my face and let the rain wash cool over my burning skin, my sister beside me. For a long time we knelt like that, with the rain running down our faces, until I felt her begin to shake.

"Let's go." We helped each other to our feet.

Back in the hospital, we found a washroom and cleaned up. I used one of the stalls.

When I came out again, Hannah was gone.

I collapsed against the wall and sank to the floor, crying. Crying for Hannah, for Dad, for myself. Crying because there was nothing left to do but cry.

After a while, I went back and sat down beside Caryn in the waiting room. "She left," I said. "She'll be okay. She'll come back."

Caryn nodded. She looked at me with frightened eyes.

"Won't she?" I asked.

We sat. We couldn't sit. We walked around. We sat some more. We watched the clock, the second hand jumping forward, second by second. We watched the doors. Turned to look for Hannah whenever they opened for someone else.

We watched people move up and down the cold hallway, listened for echoes.

We waited. The space of waiting was a fragment.

Sometime in the early hours of the morning when the dark wild night had turned calm, a doctor came.

I watched him walk toward us, I felt him lead us to a small room away from the rest of the world. My heart started thumping, louder and louder, invading the space in my head until only the space between heartbeats remained. The doctor moved and spoke in that space, framed by heartbeats and the blood on his clothes.

Thump, thump. Thump, thump. Dad was in intensive care, stable for the time being, but still in critical condition.

Thump, thump. Multiple trauma. Ruptured spleen. Compound fracture of the femur.

Thump, thump. Head injury. Skull fracture. He was unconscious. The CT scan showed some bruising, swelling.

Thump, thump. Good news, though — he was breathing on his own. They were monitoring respiration and blood-oxygen, watching for danger signs.

Thump, thump. Thump, thump. Caryn's voice. "What kind of danger?" *Thump, thump.* Danger of bleeding that would put pressure on his brain. Squeeze off its own blood supply.

Thump, thump.

An entire fragment of heartbeats and words.

24

We were able to see him. I didn't recognize the person on the bed as my father. His face was bruised and cut, one eye hidden beneath his swollen skin. His head was bandaged. Blood seeped through the white gauze, filling the tiny square weaves, one after the other. A thin trickle of blood down the side of his face was beginning to dry. There was a maze of intravenous lines and monitor cables that snaked down along the bed and disappeared under the blanket by his arm.

It would be better if we got some rest, they said. Here, if we wanted, or at home. They would call if there was any change.

Caryn nodded yes to everything and then touched me on the arm. "Hannah hasn't come back," she said, looking at Dad on the bed. "But I can't leave him now."

I nodded. She needs me, I thought. Dad needs me. How can I leave him? "Let me call home. Maybe Hannah went home."

But no one answered the phone, there or at Mom's place. Of course not, I thought, remembering that Mom was in New Orleans.

I had a vivid mental picture, suddenly, of Dad getting into his car the last time he left for B.C. Caryn stood beside the open car door; I sat on the hood. Dad paused, looked up. Hannah was slouched on the front porch, her hands in the pockets of her shorts. They looked at each other, Hannah and Dad. Caryn's hand rested on Dad's hand resting on the door frame.

I took Caryn's keys and drove home after she promised to call if there was any change at all in Dad's condition. I tried not to think too much. I concentrated on moving, on walking to the car, opening the door, sliding behind the wheel, turning the ignition on, turning the windshield wipers on, putting the car into gear. I concentrated on driving along the wet roads, making slow, careful turns, staying below the speed limit.

Light and shadow chased each other in my side vision. Lights flowed in streams through the night, colored currents of red, blue, green, white, green, white. Light flowed into shadow, shadow dissolved into light, dissolved into rain.

I parked the car squarely in the center of the garage and turned off the ignition. The dark, empty house shuddered as the garage door closed.

Hannah had been there and gone. Her note was lying on the counter, next to the dried, sticky mess of pumpkin guts.

One more fragment.

Something inside me exploded when I read Hannah's note. Anger, fear, a desperate need for life to stop tilting around me — all churned together in the pit of my stomach and erupted.

I hurled the car keys across the room with all the force I had. They gouged a cluster of holes in the wall. The room started to swim through the tears in my eyes and I slumped into a kitchen chair, crying for the second time that night.

What right did she have, pulling a stunt like this now, when Dad was fighting to stay alive? Who did she think she was? Didn't we have enough to worry about without trying to track her down, too? This time she had gone too far.

I let the sobs choke their way out and the tears fall. There was no one to see. I cried for a long time before I got up to get the box of tissues and blow my nose. And then I cried a while longer, sitting at the table with sore, puffy eyes, runny nose, aching throat, exhausted heart — and the dry, steely aftertaste of hate in my mouth.

Eventually I went to the bathroom to wash my face. My body ached. I forced myself to get up, make a cup of tea, and sip it slowly. I stood at the window, shaking and shivering. There was no way I could sleep. I walked out into the back yard and stood on the deck, taking in the night like a tonic.

The pre-dawn world was dark and still, perfectly silent, gathering itself for a morning just beginning to streak the eastern sky. A mist from the night's rain lingered in the air, cool against my hot face.

There was no frost growing on roof tops. No northern lights playing tag across the sky. No nighthawks flying above my head.

The sudden pain in my chest made me gasp. Why did I miss them so much? They were only birds. Goatsuckers, yet.

Dark and empty. Even the few stars twinkling between wisps of clouds began to fade as the sky paled.

It was my move, and the world waited.

I read Hannah's note again. *"I couldn't take waiting like that . . . I have to DO something."*

I understood that. I wanted to do something too, if only to keep from thinking about Dad, and stop feeling so helpless about everything.

Dad was lying in the hospital and Hannah was gone.

There wasn't much I could do about either.

Can't you? The pieces are there. Not everything though, not the whole story, I argued with myself.

You'll never know the whole story; you know enough. Choose. I hate this! I hate her for doing this! I should be with Dad.

Are you her sister or not? I'm her half-sister.

Words. Who else does she have? She doesn't want me! She ran away from us, didn't she? She's okay without me. She's just like . . .

Like who?

Like Mom.

Run, run as fast as you can. You can't catch me, I'm the gingerbread man. Who's the gingerbread man?

I am. We all are. Running.

So stop running and catch her. How? *Think!*

Her box.

I took the stairs two at a time and almost kicked open the door to Hannah's room. There was a pile of wet clothes on the floor. She must have changed while she was home. That was a good sign, wasn't it?

Where did she go?!

I moved quickly, scrambled under the bed for the box, found it, opened it, dumped the contents on the bed.

The knife I tossed on the floor, and the ribbons and other souvenirs I pushed aside. I went through the papers — the letters, postcards, notes, school papers, legal documents. One by one, I unfolded and read them. I read them all, frantically at first, then more carefully, sorting them as I went, remembering.

Remembering the pieces of Hannah's story, some of them for the first time. Pieces like the science fair. For me the science fair was just an evening I had to share Mom with Hannah and Peter. But now the words of Hannah's report jumped out at me. *They found out in 1925 that blood type was inherited from your parents.* And suddenly I saw Hannah checking and double-checking our blood samples under the microscope and heard her voice catch as she said, *"Type O it is. Most likely, that is."*

The notes from Natalie, the letter from school. She must have dug that out of the garbage after Dad tore it up, taped the pieces together. How was she going to tape together the broken fragments of tonight?

The drawing she'd made of herself singing in the moon. Dad had kept it on the fridge for months. I'd never seen her imaginary obituary assignment before, but reading it, I knew what she'd been thinking. And another assignment, a story she wrote when she was much younger. I'd never seen it before either. She'd called it, "One Day." But one day never happened; her story hadn't come true.

Mom's postcard. *Wish you were here.* I remembered. Hannah balanced on the edge of the roof. The sarcasm in her voice when she said, *"Don't you ever wonder why we're so different, Kel?"* And another time on the roof, after the wedding. *"What they don't know can't hurt me."*

But it can. And it did.

The thank you card with Marge's note. *If there is anything I can do to help you.* A stranger made that offer. I never did until it was almost too late. A stranger saw something in Hannah I never knew was there.

The box contained fragments, bits and pieces of Hannah's life. All part of her story. Different people with their own versions of Hannah. The version she showed them. The version they expected to see. Which was it? Maybe both. None of them saw the complete person, the real Hannah.

Was there even such a thing? Who was my sister to me? Reading the pieces of her story, I saw her better than ever before. Not all there was to see. But more than before.

Enough.

The blue-bronze sheen of the knife caught my eye. Hot knifing, Kyle had called it. They heat the hash by sticking the blade of the knife in the fire, and then inhale the fumes. There was a lot of Hannah's story I still didn't know; things I'd deliberately tried not to know. Even what I *did* know hardly seemed real.

Like Dad not being Hannah's father. And Hannah and I being half-sisters.

What was real and clear and certain was that my chest hurt and my insides cramped when I thought of Hannah and Dad, both of them lost and wandering on their own out there when they belonged with each other. And me.

What was real and certain was that Hannah belonged to Dad every bit as much as I did. None of what had happened changed that fact one iota, just like it didn't change the fact that Hannah was my sister. Or that I loved my sister, my dad and my mother. It only made them more fragile, more human.

More precious.

I picked up the last few notes from Natalie and read them again, trying to understand what they might mean. The paper shook in my hands; my body trembled uncontrollably.

H

I tried to tell you. If you're smart, you'll make a deal with him to do this one more thing and then maybe, maybe he'll leave you alone. The holiday is just too good to pass up. He needs you. If you come through who knows?

Hannah

Nat gave me your
message. Always knew you
were smart. Saturday
night then. Nat will
let you know where. Just
dont blow it.
   By the way, glad to
hear your friend didn't
get hurt. This time
       D

25

I sat on Hannah's bed and I read the notes, horrified, as I realized that Kyle's accident wasn't an accident at all. That Hannah was out there with people who could do something like this.

My heart was racing and my mouth was dry. I hugged myself, trying to stop shaking. Whatever else was still a confused blur, there was one thing I *did* know — Hannah needed help.

I stuffed the notes into my jeans' pocket and drove back to the hospital. I was pretty much running on adrenalin now. When I got there, Dad was having more tests done. Caryn came out to the waiting area and listened quietly while I told as much of the story as I knew. My version of it anyway. Hannah would have to tell her own version when we found her. I showed Caryn the notes and the clipping.

"She called," Caryn said.

"What? When?"

"She called the hospital earlier, asking about her dad."

"So there is something going on, otherwise she'd be here! She didn't just take off!" I was still explaining when, over Caryn's shoulder, I saw the doctor come out of Dad's room and walk toward us. I stopped in mid-sentence. My already racing heart began to gallop inside my chest.

Dad's respiration rate was too slow. His breathing was too shallow. They had inserted a tube down his throat to help him breathe and done another CT scan. There was some blood collection in the temporal lobe of his brain. They were flying him to the neuro ICU in Calgary.

The next thing I knew, we were watching Dad being wheeled on a stretcher down the hall and out the door. We stood there long enough to see the helicopter take off into a clear blue sky. Morning had arrived unnoticed. The pavement was steaming as last night's rain began to evaporate in the bright sunshine.

"Okay," Caryn said, turning to me. "Let's find her and then get ourselves to Calgary." I had a sudden glimpse of why Caryn and Dad were together.

We started by phoning Natalie, Lisa and Kyle. No one answered at Natalie's place. Neither Lisa or Kyle had heard from her.

Kyle immediately offered to check the regular hang-outs.

"Maybe you shouldn't." I told him about the notes and what I thought they meant. He sounded puzzled at first. "The hit-and-run driver? It wasn't an accident?"

"It was this David guy!" I almost shouted. "He's the one who almost hit you, Kyle! He was threatening Hannah, to make her help them again."

There was silence on the other end.

"Kyle?"

"Holy —"

"Maybe you shouldn't be asking around."

"Don't worry. There'll be lots of people."

"Be careful, Kyle."

It felt good to be doing something, anything. We drove by Mom's place. Even though Mom wasn't home, Hannah and I knew where the extra key was hidden. But Hannah wasn't there. Caryn gave me a weak, wry smile as we got back in the car and said, "Remind me to get you both cell phones when this is over."

We stopped at the nursing home. Marge was off for the holiday weekend, but Mr. Fletcher was sitting in a chair, staring out the window. As I got closer to him, I hesitated. He was lost in his thoughts. I wasn't sure he would recognize me.

"Mr. Fletcher, do you remember me? Kelly? Hannah's sister?"

He looked up and nodded vaguely. He seemed more disoriented than I remembered him. I introduced Caryn, then licked my dry lips and asked, "Mr. Fletcher, have you seen Hannah today?"

The question roused him, brought him back from wherever his mind was wandering. "Chickie girl? She's not come today. Said she would though. Said she would visit me on the holiday, and she will." He gave me a sharp look. "Is something wrong?"

I started to tell him, but I found myself blubbering, getting my words mixed up. I collapsed on the chair while Caryn carefully explained, telling him about Dad's accident and Hannah's disappearance.

"She was very upset, Mr. Fletcher. If you see her, would you tell her that we're looking for her? We need to find her before . . ."

Mr. Fletcher nodded. "I'll tell her. I hope he's okay, your husband."

The tears were starting to well up in Caryn's eyes, too. She managed a nod. "Thank you."

It was well past noon when we arrived home again, hoping to find Hannah there. The house was still empty. The pumpkin guts were stuck fast to the counter. Caryn automatically began to clean up the mess. I watched her for a minute and then went over to help. It took us a while, working together, to scrape off the fibres.

When the kitchen was clean, we both had a quick shower and changed clothes, then sat down to a sandwich and coffee.

The kitchen was bright with sunshine. The clouds were gone and the sky was pure blue. It should be grey and threatening outside, I thought. The sunshine just made everything seem more unreal.

Caryn phoned the hospital in Calgary. "He's still

unconscious, but he's breathing on his own again," she said when she hung up. "They've put something called a bolt into his skull to monitor the pressure on his brain."

"How . . .?" I started to ask, and then realized what the answer must be.

Caryn closed her eyes and murmured quietly. "They drilled a small hole in his skull for the bolt."

I started to cry again. I couldn't seem to stop crying. "I want to be with him," I sobbed.

"We'll get there," Caryn said, the tears shining in her eyes. She wiped them away. "I think it's time we talked to the police."

Caryn was on the phone with the police when the door bell rang. It was Kyle, looking miserable and reporting that he hadn't been able to find Hannah. No one had seen her. "Is your dad going to be okay?" he asked.

My eyes blurred and my throat tightened when I tried to answer. "We don't know yet."

"Hannah will be going crazy," he said. "We've got to find her."

Caryn hung up the phone. "The police want me to bring in the notes and a picture of Hannah. They'll start watching for her, but there's not much else they can do right now. Do either of you know who this David person is? Do you know what his last name might be?"

I tried to think. "No. I have no idea."

Kyle shook his head. "I never met the guy. Natalie would know."

Caryn nodded. "The police are going to send someone by her place."

I ran upstairs to get Hannah's latest school photo from her room. I thought I glimpsed something on the floor out of the corner of my eye, but when I turned, it was just her pile of wet clothes. I grabbed the photo from her mirror and took it to Caryn.

She slipped it into her purse. "Do you want to come along, or maybe Kyle could keep you company here in case Hannah shows up?"

Kyle nodded at me.

"We'll stay here," I said.

Caryn nodded. "Maybe you could try to reach your mom."

I didn't know where Mom was staying in New Orleans, but I knew she checked her messages when she was away. I called and left her a message to phone me as soon as possible. "Dad's been in an accident, Mom, and Hannah . . . we don't know where Hannah is. She's been gone since last night."

I hung up, then on impulse called Peter's place. I started to explain, but the words kept getting caught in my throat. Peter didn't need to hear much, though.

"Kelly, hang in there, okay? I'll track down your mom. I'll get back to you soon."

But the afternoon passed and Caryn didn't come back, and Peter didn't call. I heated up some leftovers for Kyle and me to eat for dinner, but I didn't have the stomach to eat more than a few forkfuls.

"What's keeping Caryn? Should I phone the police?"

"It's only been a couple of hours. It just seems like forever," Kyle said. "Let's wait a while longer."

"I just want to do something!" I wandered around downstairs, and then I wandered upstairs and stood in the doorway of Hannah's room. There was her softest-ever, almost buried under the wet clothes that were starting to smell. I picked the clothes up gingerly, and folded Hannah's blanket on her bed. I remember thinking that I should throw her clothes in the laundry.

I started to do just that, and then I saw the corner of a soggy piece of paper sticking out of her jacket pocket.

Careful as I was, when I pulled the paper out it came apart in my hands.

Kyle and I taped the two pieces together, but even then, the ink was so smeared it took us some time to figure out what it said.

26

"Do you think . . . " Kyle looked at me, the color gone from his face. "Should we call the police?"

"If the police pick them up, won't Hannah be charged, too? Maybe we can catch up to her ourselves. It's not quite seven. We have enough time to get there."

"This might not have anything to do with tonight."

"If she's not there, then we come home again."

Kyle shook his head, but he was smiling. "I'm beginning to see the family resemblance after all."

I stopped short. Did I know what I was getting myself into? I had taken one little step and suddenly I was knee deep in Hannah's mess. I took a deep breath. "All or nothing, I guess."

I scribbled a note to Caryn, we grabbed our jackets

and ran out the door, only to have to wait anxiously by the bus stop for almost half an hour. By the time we stepped off the bus in front of the Dairy Queen, it was after eight. And it was dark.

The bus pulled away and we ran into the restaurant. I scanned the faces of the fast food crowd. Groups of teenagers, families, older couples eating ice cream. No Hannah.

Kyle pulled on my arm and pointed to the window on the other side of the restaurant. "There!"

Hannah was getting into a car with Natalie and an older boy I'd never seen. David, I thought. We tore through the restaurant in time to watch the car pull out of the parking lot.

I don't know what we thought we were going to do if we caught them. I wasn't thinking that far ahead. I was just consumed with the idea that I had to catch Hannah. No matter what, I had to find her. I had to tell her about Dad. She would want to be with him.

Kyle threw his arms up and groaned in frustration. "Now what!"

All or nothing.

"You call the police," I said. "Let them know which way they were going and what they're driving. Did you get a look at the car?"

Kyle nodded. "It was a Ford. Just like the car that almost hit me. Only it wasn't green. It was brown."

"Go. Tell them."

"What are you going to do?"

I really didn't know, but I was already moving, jogging along the sidewalk. If I could just keep the tail lights in sight, maybe I'd be able to follow Hannah. It was dumb, but it was all I could think of.

"Kelly! Don't be stupid!" Then the car turned a corner and I ducked through the alley to head it off. Kyle and his warning were left behind.

This wasn't a cross-country race. It wouldn't do any good to pace myself. To keep the tail light in sight, I had to run, flat out.

I lasted about five minutes.

By then, the car had stopped at a traffic light two long blocks ahead of me. As soon as the light changed, I was going to lose it. Gasping for breath, my lungs burning, I slowed to a jog and then fell against a sign at the entrance to the city park that ran along the main road.

The light changed. I scanned the traffic, looking for the brown car I was following. And then there it was, turning the corner and traveling between the park and the ritzy residential area that bordered it.

I headed through the park, jogging now, slowed down by the uneven ground, dodging flower-beds and keeping one eye out for gopher holes. It was a miracle, the first of many that night, that I didn't twist an ankle. But by the time I made it back to the city streets, there was no sign of the car.

I stopped to catch my breath, trying to think. The car must have turned into one of the side streets. But which one? There was no way to tell. All I could do was check each of them in turn.

This time I paced myself — forced myself to take deep, even breaths, and found my legs settling into a steady rhythm. I ran a block into the subdivision, then turned down a street that ran parallel with the park. As I ran, I glanced down alleys and driveways.

After twenty minutes I was almost ready to give up. There didn't seem to be any way I was going to find the car. It might not even have stopped in this area. And then, passing the entrance to a back alley, I spotted a familiar dark shape halfway down, crowded up against a fence.

As quietly as possible I crept forward, staying close to the line of back yard fences. Most of them were brick or concrete, and all of them rose high above my head. The night seemed so black; clouds covered most of a crescent moon that hung over the tree tops. Up in the moon . . . There was a streetlight in the back alley, but it wasn't lit for some reason. The sudden crunch of glass under my feet brought me up short. I looked up at a jagged hole in the streetlight above me.

No one seemed to have heard the sound, so I started toward the car again, crouching low behind the rear end. It was the brown Ford. Empty.

But when I flattened myself against the fence and held perfectly still, I could just make out quiet whispers coming from the yard on the other side, the shuffle of a foot on a hard surface.

There was a gate in the fence. It was shut and the latch was on the inside. They must have climbed over somehow, I thought. How? The fence was well above my head. There was no way over that I could see. Unless —

The metal gave beneath my feet as I crawled onto

the hood of the Ford and carefully stepped up on its roof. I didn't care if I left dents, as long as I didn't make any sound that would give me away.

Slowly, cautiously, I straightened up enough to peer over the fence into the dark back yard. I froze.

The thin beam of a flashlight was pointed at the ground near a small basement window. Someone stumbled and swore. Someone else hissed, "Shut up! Get on with it."

As my eyes adjusted to the dark, I could make out three people huddled close to the house, hidden from the neighboring houses on both sides by thick bushes.

I strained to hear what they were whispering, but I couldn't catch any of the words. The flashlight gave off just enough light for me to see one of the dark shapes pry open the window. When it was open as far as it would go, the person stepped back.

Hannah lay flat on her belly, squirmed under the open windowpane, and disappeared inside. That's why they needed her, I realized. Anyone bigger would never have fit through such a small opening.

A minute later the back door opened and Hannah stepped out. She began walking across the patio but David grabbed her arm.

"That's it," she hissed at him. "I got it open for you. Now I'm out of here."

I held my breath.

"I don't think so. There's still stuff to carry out to the car. You can help." He pulled her back and shoved her roughly into the house ahead of him. I winced. This was a guy who tried to drive over people if you ticked him off. He was dangerous, and he had Hannah.

I searched desperately for some idea. Maybe if I distracted them somehow, it would give Hannah a chance to run. But how?

They were coming out of the house now, each of them carrying something. I ducked and clambered down as quietly as I could in my hurry. There was no place to hide! I scuttled back to the streetlight and crouched behind it, counting on the shadows to hide me.

The gate opened and something rustled in the bushes. An animal scooted by me. It was all I could do not to cry out. The three shapes froze, blending almost perfectly into the night.

"What was that?"

Silence.

One of the shapes moved again — Natalie, walking to the back of the car and opening the trunk. "Nothing. Just a cat."

They made another trip into the house. From what I could see, they had taken a video camera, VCR, CD players, discs, radios and even a small TV. The trunk closed with a click. Time was running out.

"Okay. I'm leaving now," Hannah whispered.

David and Natalie looked at each other. "You know," said David, his voice hard and quiet, "something tells me you can't quite be trusted. I think I'd feel better if you stuck with us until we unload this stuff. You want your money, don't you?"

Hannah started edging around the other side of the car. "Keep it. I just want to go see my dad."

"Gee, I'm sorry. But you're going to have to wait."

Suddenly, everything happened at once.

I was tired of these bullies. I was going to see my father, and so was Hannah. I don't know where I got the nerve, except that I was exhausted, functioning on pure adrenalin, and nearly hysterical.

I stood up, stepped into the alley and cleared my throat, hoping to make my voice sound more threatening. I was going to say, "No. She's not waiting."

Just as I opened my mouth, sirens screamed and blue and red lights flashed everywhere. They were on all sides of me it seemed, everywhere I looked. Police cars sped into the alley from both ends. Trapped, everyone froze like deer in the glare of headlights.

Except me. My mouth closed, my legs gave out and I sank to my knees, faint with relief.

27

The police station was swarming — not confused and noisy, but quietly and efficiently swarming. People moved by us, others sat on chairs in a waiting area. The drone of activity was interrupted regularly by the phone ringing.

An officer showed us to a room and suddenly everyone was talking at once. Everyone being me, Hannah and Kyle. And then the door opened and Caryn and Mr. Fletcher, of all people, walked in.

"Did we nab 'em, Chickie?" Fletch grinned.

"Thanks to you, old man." Hannah gave him a tired smile and a slow high five.

"Not so old as all that, girl."

Hannah just smiled, too tired to come back with

another quip. Caryn looked bewildered; she hugged Hannah and me, tight, and kept shaking her head. Kyle was so excited he couldn't sit still.

"I don't believe you ran after that car," he kept saying. "I just don't believe it."

It didn't take long to figure out that it was Mr. Fletcher who had phoned the police with a tip about a certain hit-and-run driver and a possible break-and-enter in the Parkview Estates area. Information that Hannah had given him when she'd gone to see him that afternoon.

"You could have called me," Kyle pouted. "I would've helped you."

Hannah shook her head. "Sure. They'd already threatened you once. But they didn't know about Mr. Fletcher."

Kyle's phone call from the Dairy Queen alerted the police to the general location of the car they were looking for, and they spotted it parked in the alley soon after.

"Why didn't you just stand up to David and Natalie?" I asked Hannah while Caryn was talking to an officer.

"I didn't know what they might do," she said. "Besides, I wanted them to get caught, and they would've called it all off if I hadn't shown up." Her face turned hard and determined. "I found out it was Natalie who arranged to have me turned in to the police the first time. They wanted to find out if I could be trusted."

I shuddered. "Remind me not to tick you off."

"It was worth it to see your face when the lights and sirens started up. Never in my wildest dreams did I imagine that my knight in shining armor would be my sister!"

"You knew the police were going to turn up!" I could feel my cheeks burning. Talk about feeling stupid! Big sister to the rescue. Some rescue. What was I thinking? Somehow, though, I was still glad that I did it, even if it was kind of melodramatic.

"Well," Hannah said. "I hoped they would, anyway. I thought there was a pretty good chance. But I had to be there, too, or David and Natalie would have known. You showing up, though. That beats everything."

Kyle broke in, blurting out the question I didn't want to ask. "Won't you get charged, too?"

Hannah sighed, suddenly serious again. "If I do, it was worth it to get these guys off my back." She turned to me. "Kel, how's Dad?"

I looked at Caryn.

"No change," said Caryn. "I think he could use a cheering section. Let's get over there."

"We can go?" I jumped up. "Hannah, too?"

"Mr. Fletcher and Kyle can stay and give their statements now. We'll come back to give ours later." She turned to Mr. Fletcher. "When this is all over, you are going to be our guest for dinner one night. You too, Kyle. We can't begin to thank you both enough."

Mr. Fletcher bowed low, dignified. "It would be an honor to dine with your family."

"Oh, Fletch," said Hannah. She threw her arms around him. "You're such a suck. But you're in for a treat. Caryn is a great cook."

I don't know who was more stunned, Caryn or me.

The three of us swept out of the police station and piled into Caryn's car.

"Is Dad all right?" Hannah asked again.

"He's in Calgary, Hannah," Caryn explained. "We're going there now. Now that you're safe." She paused and added, "He's going to be so terribly proud of you."

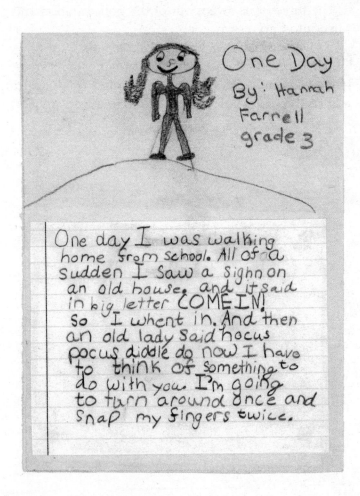

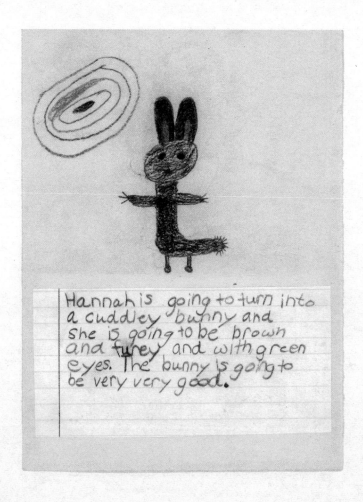

Hannah is going to turn into
a cuddley bunny and
she is going to be brown
and furey and with green
eyes. The bunny is going to
be very very good.

The bunny is going to run every ware. She will run to the zoo and to my friend's house and to the store. At night the bunny will sleep in my bed all cutled up in my soft tsed ever.

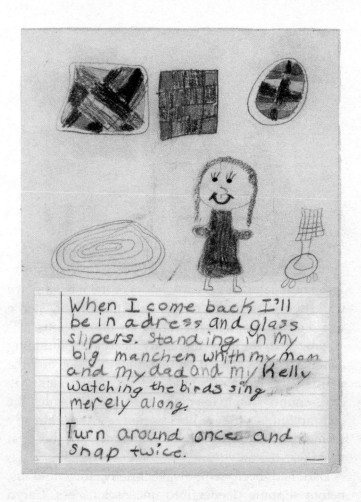

When I come back I'll
be in a dress and glass
slipers. Standing in my
big manchen whithmymom
and my dad and my Kelly
watching the birds sing
merely along.

Turn around onces and
snap twice.

28

Two hours later, in the early hours of the morning, we walked out of the darkness into the bright, sterile world of the hospital where Dad lay unconscious.

Now that we were there, my heart was pounding again. My steps echoed on the shiny tile floor, and the whir of the elevator sounded loud in my ears. My cross-country run in the night, the break-and-enter, the commotion at the police station — they already seemed to belong to another lifetime. The hospital room was the only reality.

Dad had been semi-awake briefly, they told us, before slipping deeper into unconsciousness. Caryn was sitting on one side of the bed, Hannah and I were standing on the other side. Caryn picked up Dad's hand and held it in her own, rubbing the back of his hand gently.

She leaned forward. "Ian? We're here. We're all here."

He didn't move.

"Dad?" Hannah said, ever so softly.

Dad, she had said.

His eyes stayed closed.

We stayed with him for a long time. Hours. The nurses came and went. The doctors came and went. Dad sank deeper into unconsciousness. Some time during the day I heard the words, "subdural hematoma . . . bleeding in the temporal lobe."

There was no change all that day. At one point, Caryn dug something out of a bag and put it on the table beside Dad's bed. It was a picture of him with his arms wrapped around Hannah and me.

We took turns catching a little rest. Except for dozing during the drive to Calgary, I hadn't slept in two days. As exhausted as we were, none of us could really sleep now, either. Hannah wandered back and forth, staring out the window, then standing beside Dad's bed. I sat down in one of the chairs in the corner of the room, too weary to stand any longer. My eyes closed.

A soft murmur woke me some time later. Hannah's voice, quietly reciting in the dim fading light of dusk. "On Saturday night I lost my dad, and where do you think I found him? Up in the moon, singing a tune, with all the stars around him."

Hannah and I were alone with Dad. Caryn must have left the room for a few minutes. Hannah was holding Dad's hand, her eyes bright with tears. I got up and stood beside her, not sure what else to do. She leaned her head on my shoulder and then I was crying with her.

"I don't want him to die, Kelly. It's the first thing I've been sure of in months."

"He's not going to die," I whispered fiercely. "He's not."

Hannah blinked and wiped her eyes with the back of her hand. "When I ran out of the hospital," she said, "I didn't know where I was going, I didn't care. All I could think of was him, lying there. Dying. My father was dying. All those months he was Ian, because it hurt less when he was Ian. But suddenly he was my father again. How could that be, Kelly?"

It was too much to think about. My head hurt. I was in so much agony of my own; how could I possibly face Hannah's pain right now? But she was my sister. I ached for her, almost as much as for the still figure lying on the bed.

"Do you know that you can't just up and stop loving people, no matter how much it hurts? Even when you want to. And I didn't want to anymore. All I wanted was to be his daughter. That's all I ever wanted. Even when I was so angry at Mom and Dad, I couldn't stand to look at them."

"Where did you go?"

"I went home and changed out of my wet clothes, walked some more. Slept in the school yard, in the playground tunnels." She smiled, remembering. "Nearly scared the daylights out of two little kids in the morning. After I managed to convince them I wasn't a sex pervert, I wandered around again until I figured out what to do about David and Natalie." She looked at me. "I called the hospital, to make sure Dad was okay."

I nodded.

"I don't know who I am. I'm not even sure a person can ever know something like that. But I didn't want Natalie and David telling me who I was going to be, what I was going to do. I could at least make that choice."

Caryn came back into the room and quietly stood at the foot of Dad's bed.

Hannah sat down on the edge of the bed. She leaned over and ever so lightly kissed Dad's cheek. "Up in the moon, singing a tune," she whispered. "Please come back to earth, Dad."

I looked at Hannah and Dad through swimming eyes. Teary stars shuddered and broke around them.

My heart was so full of so many things. I reached out and brushed the hair back over the bandages on Dad's forehead, leaned down and kissed him, whispering, "I love you, too, Dad."

Still looking at him, I added, "I'm so glad you're my sister, Hannah."

She sniffed and wiped her eyes. And she nodded. "Ditto." Then she looked over at Caryn. "You too, Caryn. I'm glad you were there . . . Thanks. I know I've been pretty rotten."

"You were dealt a rotten hand," Caryn said. "What's important is that we are all here now, together."

I think that's what a real family does, somehow becomes stronger and better when things are worse. Mom arrived with Peter toward evening and we all kept watch over Dad together. Every extra person made me feel stronger.

In the middle of the night, the pressure on Dad's brain rose suddenly and sharply. They took him away for another CT scan. There was more bleeding. There wasn't much time, the neurosurgeon said. If they didn't operate, he would die. The pressure inside his skull was getting so high that his heart couldn't pump hard enough to get blood to his brain.

Surgery wouldn't necessarily save him, they said. He might already have suffered irreversible brain damage. Even if Dad lived, he might be a vegetable.

No guarantees.

Some choices are just too hard to make.

But you have to make them anyway. The three of us made our choice, together, supported by each other and by Mom and Peter, and all the doctors and nurses.

It was Thanksgiving day, although none of us remembered it at the time.

The surgery went as well as could be expected, the doctor told us after.

Dad woke up four days later. He opened his eyes. He knew who we were.

He squeezed my hand ever so slightly, and he looked at Hannah and his eyes blinked slowly and his cracked lips tried to form a smile that came out all skewed around the tube in his mouth.

29

It's early, but I convince Hannah that this is the best time to be outside. We try not to disappoint each other too much these days and so she crawls out of bed and walks with me into a deep silent shroud of fog. The sun is just beginning to dissolve the higher edges. On the ground we can see our feet against the first white skiff of snow, and a few steps in front. But the alley ahead is vague and then disappears completely.

It is easy to wander a few steps off the gravel and into the field.

Past a weather-beaten fencepost tilting curiously over a slight depression, Hannah stoops suddenly and peers at something by her feet, brushing away the snow with the cuff of her jacket. Says she thinks it's a nighthawk. I squat beside her and we stare at the broken, stiff form. We wonder what happened. Its bones are broken, its feathers shredded, its body already mingling with the soil.

Nighthawks nest on the ground, I remember. Maybe, we think, maybe the bird was confused by the combine and flew off in the wrong direction. End of story for this nighthawk. But when I stand over the dead bird's body and close my eyes, I can see the nighthawk flying above me. I see long pointed wings beating — slow, powerful. Then suddenly erratic. *Flapflap . . . flap . . . flapflapflap . . . flapflap.* The bird gyrates wildly upward. Harsh, piercing calls punctuate its climb. I see the dark fleck move crazily in the sky, then stop, poised above the world. I see it plummet, hear the wind singing through its wings, a quivering hum, as the bird drops from clear heights to dissolve in the earth's shadows. I hear the vibrating buzz accelerate into a swooping crescendo. And end. Out of the shadows the nighthawk arcs skyward and begins another wild gyrating climb into the dying light.

When I open my eyes, I can't see through the fog. But I can feel a rustle moving out of the mist toward us. The bird is dead, but I can feel it in the sky, sense its energy like an electric current running through my body. "Feel it," I tell Hannah. Closer and closer, almost above us now; slow powerful beats, muffled whistling wings.

The geese emerge like a vision conjured from the mist; dissolve back into mist. "It's the geese flying south," laughs Hannah. Her laugh hangs in the air, wrapped in mist.

And she's right, it is the geese. But the nighthawk is there, too. Within the geese, within Hannah, within me. Within Dad.

They will be back.

Dad, too, will be back. He's already halfway there and he'll make it all the way, even if the doctors say they don't know how far that is. We can wait. Because his presence is already strong here in our home and it won't be long before the rest of him follows.

He will be different. He may not be a welder anymore. Can't tell yet. He can talk a little, though, and understand as much as anyone. He'll get better with therapy.

He is alive. His story has only changed direction. All our stories have changed direction. My story includes the photo club again, and the cross-country team, maybe a movie with Sean one Saturday. It's only a date, Erin says. I think I'm ready to tell her the story.

The mist is dissolving and we walk through it, past the field to the little pond where the fog is still beautiful, steaming on the water as the sun soaks it up. Breathy wisps slide across the pond's glassy surface.

I watch Hannah out of the corner of my eye because she is also alive again. Her story has changed, too, maybe more than anyone's. This newfound sister, quietly older, who spent a wet cold night curled against the plastic curve of a playground tunnel and crawled out again holding onto the pieces of herself.

Her story turns out to be about Humpty Dumpty,

not Peter Pan, and the pieces can't be put back together again; or they can, but not in the same way, because the piece that was her and the piece that was me and all of the pieces, it seems, have changed shape. They have a different, less comfortable fit and they make a new story.

In her courtroom chapter, Hannah is now a witness, not a defendant. She has another father, not mine. She's going to save that story, she says, for later. Not for long, but not now. Dad is all the father she needs for now.

Telling Hannah's story made it my story, too. Because the shape that emerged as I told it was my own, and the discovery changed me. But the story is not over yet. Hannah's. Mine. There are so many different beginnings . . . Another one is now.

Here. This morning. This pond. This moment.

Hannah's laugh, the color of cotton candy wisps of fog melting on the warm breath of sunshine.